Nakba

The Civilizing War Volume I

by Jason S. Walters

I0683832

a BlackWyrm book
Louisville, Kentucky

NAKBA
The Civilizing War Volume 1

By Jason S. Walters
Copyright © by BlackWyrm Games

A BlackWyrm Book
BlackWyrm Publishing
10307 Chimney Ridge Ct, Louisville, KY 40299

ISBN: 978-1-61318-145-4

ABOUT JASON S. WALTERS

For *The Vast White*

"I was extremely impressed with [the Vast White] – it's funny, extremely well written, highly original, and has some really terrific innovations." — John O-Neill, *Black Gate*

"Jason Walters has a bloodhound's nose for story, a jeweler's eye for detail and a healthy appreciation of the joys of history, both true and certainly-should-be-true." — Darren Watts, *Millennium City*

"Jason Walters's work never fails to impress and intrigue me. With a voice that mixes intelligence, humor, wisdom, insight into the human condition, and gleefully barbed observations about life, he's a desert-bred cross between Hunter S. Thompson and Chris Rock who's thankfully chosen to set his sights on genre fiction rather than reporting or comedy. I'm already looking forward to his next book." — Steven S. Long, *Dark Champions*

"Sometimes the cover says it all. Desert setting. Mythological creatures. Warriors battling to the death. An overemphasis on the female anatomy. The Vast White is one for the guys." — *Tribute Books Reviews*

For *An Unforgiving Land*

"These are horror stories. But what makes them unusual and evocative is that the horrors rise right out of the rocks and sand and flora and fauna of the desert. A Judas horse, trained to help men bring in herds of mustangs, realizes it's turning its own kind into dog food — and rebels. Hunters encounter a cat that is ... well, just a little bigger and wilder than all the rest. A lonely old lady invites a pack of coyotes to do a deed that she herself cannot. Even the meth cookers are a little crazier, a little more violent, and quite a lot stranger in this bleak land. But if you've spent time in the desert you'll almost believe these things could be real." — Claire Wolfe, *www.backwoodshome.com*

"A tribute to the people of Gerlach." — *Reno Gazette Journal*

"This collection of horrific short stories from Nevada's Black Rock Desert will give you nightmares for years to come." — Dave Mattingly, *The Algernon Files*

"This book may need a warning label: a possible side effect is that your mind will become altered." — Marge Fulton, *All Roads Lead to Hazard* and *The Holler*

"The skillful structure of the stories is matched by Walter's wordcraft. He evokes the danger and beauty of the Black Rock environment in spare terms that, over time, allow the reader to get to know the place." — *RobotViking*

"In the introduction of *An Unforgiving* Land Jason explains the the book is a love story to his home and the Black Rock Desert. That is really what this is in a horrific and twisted sort of way. The tales meander to different peoples, places, and events giving the reader a bitter taste of this desolate place." — *Kingbeast's Lair*

"Eight well written but dark and stark tales of life in and around Hualapai on the Black Rock Desert." — *Alternative Worlds*

"I frickin' loved reading *An Unforgiving Land*. Like many, my introduction to the Black Rock Desert was through Burning Man. But over the years as the newness of Burning Man has waned, the call to the desert has waxed. There is something deeply American, rugged, mysterious, independent – something Cowboy that comes out in me when I visit this place. In *An Unforgiving Land* the author trapped into this resonance and took me there from the cozy confines of my Seattle condo. If, like me, you feel the call of this haunting place – with or without Burning Man – do yourself a favor and buy this book. You won't be disappointed!" — Peter Adkinson, *GenCon*

"Jason Walters' tales are violent, lustful, and more than anything else, compelling. The sex demon of Burning Man is, alone, worthy of iconic stature. At once obvious and unthinkable, she-who-cannot-be-denied is one of the great creations of contemporary literature. The stories of wacko cowboys, tattooed postmodern crazies and supernatural fauna at first appear unrelated, but they build to a narrative of place – and end-of-the-road, out-of-chances, desperate kind of place that is both the real Northwestern Nevada and a state of mind. You will never see the West the same way again. You will never hear the wind rustling in sagebrush without reaching for your gun, even though you know the shots will not save you. When you read Walters, you enter a parallel universe that leaves you creepily unsure of your own, forever." — Donald Asher, author and lecturer

For *Posthegemony: Terra Nomenklatura*

"Mr. Walters's dystopian Utopia is a great example of how to create a plausible, convincing society. It's frighteningly realistic because one can easily imagine such a world coming to pass." — James Cambias, *Terran Empire*

"I really think Jason has something special with Posthegemony." — *Kingbeast's Lair*

NAKBA

The Civilizing War Volume I

Nak-ba [*an-Nak-bah*] noun Origin: Arabic. Literally: disaster, catastrophe, or cataclysm.

1. The 1948 Palestinian exodus when approximately 700,000 Palestinian Arabs left, fled, or were expelled from their homes during the 1948 Arab-Israeli War and the Civil War that preceded it. The exact number of refugees is a matter of dispute. The causes remain the subject of fundamental disagreement between Arabs and Israelis.

2. The murder, property confiscation, deportation, and even deliberate emigration of roughly one million Sephardi and Mizrahi Jews from Arab and Islamic countries in the years and decades following the 1948 Arab-Israeli War. Called the *Jewish Nakba,* it is also a matter of historic dispute and debate between Arabs and Israelis.

3. The voluntary diaspora of countless thousands of non-conformist dissidents from the Earth into outer space during and following the establishment of Posthegemony rule over the planet. The Children of the Nakba included Jews, Arabs, and Muslims. Sometimes they fled together. Of this there is neither debate nor dispute.

BOOK ONE: A REMEMBRANCE OF HER

I felt only night within me
It was then that I conceived
The new art
> — Kasimir Malevich, *The Non-Objective World*

6:00 AM: Earth, New Reno Metro

"Stanton, it's time to wake up and prepare for work."

The man rose smoothly from his bed. He grasped a silk kimono from nearby hook, sliding it over his thin, muscular frame in a single, fluid motion. Then he walked out of his bedchamber and into the room which was the remainder of his apartment. He lit a cigarette, watching the red light at its tip thoughtfully in the gloom.

Moments passed.

"Sentience," he said after a while, exhaling a thin plume of smoke, "exterior view please: realistic, actual."

"Yes Stanton." the voice of Sentience was melodic and deep, yet still distinctively female. All four walls of the room and the ceiling vanished, replaced by a cityscape hidden by the final shreds of night. The first rays of dawn had begun to tentatively peak over the low mountains east of the city, but as of yet the crown of the rising sun hadn't made its appearance. The man continued smoking his cigarette – an Indian Beedi, made with flavored tobacco – as the sun finally rose above the dry, dusty hills. Finally, he sighed, tossing the still-smoldering butt into the sink where it laid, smoking and stinking, amidst the soggy corpses of its fellows. His daily moment of peace was at an end.

"Sentience, interior design: *Vkhutemas*, Obmas school."

The exterior cityscape was replaced with the stark, sleek lines and open spaces of modernist 1920s Soviet avaunt-garde architecture. Stanton smiled. It was, as with so many things in his life, a private joke. *Vkhutemas* – the experimental architecture of Soviet revolution – had been condemned as "abstract" and banned to make way for Stalinist Gothic; a reactionary school of architecture and interior design if there had ever been one.

He made his way back to the bedroom, rolling aside the doors of a long wardrobe built directly into the wall. It contained, in varying degrees of gray, brown, and dark blue, suits that wouldn't have looked entirely out of place on Mao Zedong or Jawaharlal Nehru: all high collars, pockets, and buttons. Today was destined to be an outdoorsy occasion, so he chose a khaki number with just a hint of "safari" in its tailoring. Then he went to the bathroom – really, just a tiny alcove on the other side of the room – where he washed his face, combed his hair, and applied cologne that had just a hint of wood to it, indicating seriousness. He applied it moderate-plus, enlarging his personal scent space as befitted his station.

The wardrobe was a personal eccentricity. His Faber could easy create newer, more fashionable clothing for him each day. However, he enjoyed the actual physical process of selecting his clothes. Running his hands idly through the fabric. Brushing the shoulder pads. Checking for rips or stains.

It was worth sacrificing five-percent of his allocated living space.

"Stanton? You have a call from Ms. Mitsuoni."

"Put it on the nearest surface if you could please."

The face of Naomi Mitsuoni, Stanton's secretary-mistress, instantly appeared on the wall next to him. A delicate Japanese Gothic Lolita ragamuffin, she was dressed in black and purple with heavy dark eyeliner. Her hair, a crazy mélange of multicolored dreadlocks, was mostly stuffed inside of an exaggerated top hat. She frowned at her employer disapprovingly.

"Mr. Wong, you *do* remember that we have a company picnic today, don't you?" she chided him in her singsong little girl voice, "The staff is *so* looking forward to going to the desert. Most of them have never been."

"Of course Ms. Mitsuoni; I was just now getting dressed. Has our... friend arrived yet?"

"Yes sir. He is here already." The two exchanged an inscrutable look. "I am making Mr. Ng comfortable pending your arrival at the factory."

"Very good. I will be there shortly." Wong waved his hand angrily, instantly severing the connection.

"Damn *nomenklatura!*" he hissed to no one in particular. The term meant, "list of names" in Old Russian, simultaneously referring to the Soviet ruling caste and the list of those favored by them. Sentience answered all the same, as was its habit.

"But Stanton, you're nomenklatura." it said in its sultry, *femme-fatale* voice.

"You don't have to remind me," he muttered darkly. "And you know better, anyhow." He stalked toward the door of his 800-square foot dwelling, snatching his medallion-like Personal Sentience from its station on the wall as he departed.

Most of his contemporaries would have considered the place to be a palace.

7:10 AM: Earth, Bay Area Metro

The sun had already risen over the bay when Zhang completed the last of the 19 movements of the *Tai Chi Chih,* effortlessly finishing with Six Healing Sounds. His hands drifted gracefully through the air while he exhaled, as if he were slowly pushing away a heavy, invisible wall. With that finished, he brought them together, palms out and fingers touching, into the Cosmic Consciousness Pose, so that the opposing energies scattered throughout his body could come back together, establishing equilibrium.

And there he stood.

The Uncarved Block, the ancient Chinese had called it, suggesting a pose of absolute wholeness and stillness. But that was an unsuitably cryptic and uncivic title for the modern era; so Cosmic Consciousness it now was. If you practiced enough, you could genuinely feel your body re-centering itself after the movements, and be gifted with an unparalleled moment of clarity. And that is what its practitioners stove for: unparalleled clarity.

Tai Chi Chih wasn't a martial art. Such things were Discouraged in the Posthegemony. It was barely even an exercise. Rather, it was a system for unifying the body with the mind, and for developing Chi: the active life-force of the body. Zhang wasn't sure if he believed in Chi or not. Certainly his ancestors had. Of course, his ancestors had also believed in flying dragon gods, the Celestial bureaucracy, and telling fortunes using hexagrams. Ancestor reverence only went so far. However, his morning exercises gave him a chance to reflect on the concerns of the day in a leisurely, and most importantly, non-suspicious manner.

Everything in Posthegemony society had to do with not being suspicious. Not being "interesting," even if you genuinely weren't up to anything. Being an Interesting Person was to be avoided at all costs. It was an ingrained, cultivated, Encouraged behavior, even in someone as hypothetically untouchable as Zhang. Usually he didn't even know he was doing it.

He stood on an ancient, weathered stone wall in the Berkeley Hills which provided a magnificent view of the Bay Area Metro below. In an earlier age it had been a popular spot for motorcyclists to stop and chat. Now it was a relic: the luxury homes that once surrounded it gone, the roads that led to it removed, and the many delights of the Tilden Regional Park demolished as if they had never existed. The Metro stopped abruptly at the base of the Berkeley Hills, its scrapers and open spaces having never been allowed to creep up its green sides to spread the disease of humanity.

He could feel a wet, chill wind blowing behind him; most likely off of Lake Anza. Unlike the vast majority of the inhabitants of the Metro he had seen, and even swum, in the lake. For Zhang was not merely nomenklatura. He was more than that.

The metro gleamed and shimmered in the morning sun beneath him, stretching across the Bay, away into the west, north, and south as far as the eye could see. He stood just beyond its eastern border, where its expansion had been halted long ago to create suitable space between it and the SacMetro some 120 kilometers away. It was a storied place: the first Metro to be established in North America. Indeed, the inhabitants of the area once known as San Francisco had welcomed the Posthegemony as liberators, allies, and fellow travelers even while the majority of the inhabitants of the continent had still imagined themselves to be citizens of the long-lost polities known as the United States, Mexico, and Canada. Though not for long. The Posthegemony was always quick to divorce people from unproductive, nationalist illusions.

This natural tendency of its populace toward proper, Encouraged thinking was what had made the Bay Area Metro is the *de facto* capital of the North American Administrative Zone, even though the WashMetro on the other side of the continent was its capital *de jure*. Well, that and the weather, which was very nearly perfect as far as Zhang – as well as most of the nomenklatura in the zone – were concerned. You just couldn't hide the fact that WashMetro was built on a swamp; a good place to send promising protégés for a little toughening up, but not for living in oneself.

Zhang's day would undoubtedly be like any other. Oh, there was a *possibility* things could get interesting. They did from time to time. But the business of protecting the producer-consumers of Earth was mostly a fairly routine and, if truth be told, boring one that left Zhang with a lot of time to think. He spent a lot of that time contemplating *governance:* that elusive, S.A.C -era buzzword which had flowed perpetually from the lips of the Posthegemony's unwitting European forefathers of the past, helping birth the far more perfectly balanced – and perpetual – society of the present from its Asian cultural midwives. In moments of whimsy, these odd men had trotted out even fancier, more magnificent names like "metagovernance" and "global governance" with meant, basically, the same thing. It meant, simply, the act of governing; well, the act of *them* governing *you*. But it sounded so much better, so much less frightening in so many different languages – especially since the word "government" itself had become a profanity by the time of the S.A.C, untrusted and unwanted by the Earth's surviving population. Government had come to mean oppression, genocide, poverty, violence, dispossession, and powerlessness. Governance was thought to be sort of *like* government... but without all the bad stuff that made government, well, government.

People who hated government loved governance, though they didn't know what it meant... or, if indeed, meant anything at all. Its nobility and utility as a word lay in its nebulousness. And, in Zhang's society, nebulousness lay at the heart of governance. Actually, it lay at the heart of everything.

"The oppressed are allowed once every few years to decide which particular representatives of the oppressing class are to represent and repress them." Karl Marx had once famously said, and the people of Zhang's era took it to heart: ironically, quasi-ironically, and completely literally. Of course unlike Marx's idealized society the Posthegemony wasn't a dictatorship of the proletariat. It wasn't a dictatorship of any kind. Actually, it was rather hard to say what the Posthegemony was, exactly: which made it all the more pernicious to those few who paid attention to such things.

There were elections, of course. Though they were obviously spectacle with less actual real world effect than a closely contested Sepak Takraw match. There were corporations that made various nice things from Slurpees to speedboats. (All of them at least partially owned by family members of the Posthegemony's vast nomenklatura: the sons, nephews, or brother-in-laws of someone important to its administration.) There were pretty stars and starlets from Hollywood, Bollywood, and Paris who championed the politically popular causes of the day. They came and went like peddles on a dying flower.

All of this was very polite and acceptable in its treacle-like sameness. Encouraged. There was no dictator, king, president, or chairman: no one for the masses (such as they were in an ultra-post-post-modern individualist society) to focus their collective hatreds on. Nor did its innumerable bureaucracies publicly have heads, even symbolic ones. Zhang's title wasn't a particularly impressive one in the grand scheme of things. Which was, of course, by design. Those attempting to penetrate the depths of one of the Posthegemony's many departments, even upon a steed of perfectly filled-out paperwork, found themselves ascending a spiraling, bureaucratic Ouroboros that invariably led them back to the same tired functionary they'd initially spoken with.

It was deliberately, scientifically infuriating, and thus not worth the limited time and energy of any reasonably sane person to deal with. Which was why most people chose instead to get a cappuccino, buy a new pair of trousers, or have sex with a Japanese robot instead. Nor in an era of nanotechnology, surplus population, and cheap cloning could it effectively be shot at, blown up, or burned down. By all means young wacko: go at a Posthegemony building with all the Timothy McVeigh *cum* Osama Bin Laden *cum* Robin Hood righteous fury you like. In a week it will just grow back, complete with the same bored, empty-eyed staff you so gleefully murdered the week before.

Terrorism has thus become as pointless as every other antisocial behavior on Earth. Which rather took all the fun out of it. *Which was rather the point,* Zhang thought.

"General Zhang," his Military Sentience chimed, its voice calm and faintly accented with antique Mandarin, "the base requests your immediate presence. Satellites have reported an antisocial emergence 2,964 kilometers to the north of the Bay Area Metro."

He dropped his Cosmic Consciousness Pose, quickly abandoning his musings.

"Initiate the standard surrender protocols," he said with an air of quiet command. "Make a detailed recording of everything that transpires, along with your analysis of the craft they've constructed. I want to know everything about it. Give them a chance to surrender; if they do, have them picked up for ReEducation. If they don't... blow their pig faces out of the sky before anyone can see them."

Then General Zhang Dakota Wannian climbed nimbly into his floater and descended toward the Metro, skimming over trees where homes once stood.

7:35 AM: Earth, New Reno Metro

Stark, crude shapes floated around the interior holosurfaces of Stanton Wong's egg-shaped Floater. Black circles and squares on white background. A black crosses intersecting a red oval. Brown and gray rectangles linked by yellow lines.

Suprematism: Russian futurist art of the distant past. A desperate attempt to pry meaning from the darkness of modern life, in which the artist's inner journey was externalized in the form of basic geometric forms. A return to purity: impossible, pretend shapes traveling through time and space. Two-dimensional painted masses in a state of movement. A desperate, doomed, and beautiful artistic gesture, nearly impossible for the authorities of the old Soviet Union to understand, and thus banned along with all other abstract art as "decadent."

He exhaled slowly in contemplation. He was fan: another obscure, personal joke.

The school was all but forgotten, buried by the sands of time like so many other strange and beautiful things for the crime of being boring to the modern masses. *The old Soviets were so crude,* he thought. *Better to hide the unwanted from public sight through indifference, rather than censorship.* That way the velvet glove need never come off the iron fist of the state.

Not that Stanton Wong's existence was boring or even censored: far from it. By the standards of 99% of everyone that had ever existed in every parallel dimension and in every time period that ever was, his life was fascinating, liberated, and basically kind of awesome. He was powerful, good looking, wealthy, and highly intelligent. He was also bored, disillusioned, and bitter and, in the end, that turned out to be more important to him than the abstract knowledge that he had it far better than an African-American woman in Alabama in the 1950's, a medieval French peasant in the year 807, or a Jewish shopkeeper in 1930's Berlin. The knowledge simply didn't make his life any more bearable.

He lived in New Reno, which in all honesty looked and smelled a lot better than old Reno. One of North America's many metropolitan areas – or "Metros," for short – it stretched to what had been Tahoe in the west and to Carson City in the south, looking a great deal like an ocean-sized psychedelic coral reef. It was an organic, preplanned metropolis of spotless BioCrete buildings, large parks, and very little traffic, as very few of its inhabitants could afford Floaters or eCars in any case. But some things never change in the Biggest Little Metro In The Posthegemony. The Strip was still lined with dozens of bustling casinos, each competing with the next to project the largest, most audacious holodisplays offering The Loosest Slots And Best Vfood Buffets In Town! And, in a world nearly devoid of bad smells and filth, Reno still maintained its tradition of dive bars, all of which had been painted with artificial grime and whose owners paid top dollar to have nanobacteria manufactured scents of sweat, piss, and vomit pumped out of invisible pores in the walls.

Not that Stanton Wong frequented that sort of place. He imagined that Ms. Mitsuoni, when she wasn't out with him in her official capacity as almost-underage eye candy, probably did. However, Wong was a factory owner, which automatically made him nomenklatura, depriving him of the right to slum. It was part of his social role to set an example; in fact, it was dangerous for him not to do so. He sighed and lit another Beedi. Its blue-black smoke hovered in the climate-controlled environment of his Floater, and then vanished as his Sentience pumped it outside.

"Stanton, please remember to use the ashtray. Repairing the upholstery is an unnecessary expense."

"Yeah, yeah." he muttered absently at his Sentience, currently docked into dashboard of his Floater, which was deep gray, ovular, and featureless. It hovered silently three feet above the ground, occasionally lifting a bit higher to avoid stray children, incautious bicyclists, and the odd drunken reveler. Though compact by the standards of the 20th Century, the vehicle was enormous compared to the toy-like electric cars that comprised most of New Reno's traffic. Brightly colored and boxlike, eCars were the preferred transportation of the *post-polloi:* shopkeepers, low-level bureaucrats, managers, and the like. Most people either walked or rode bicycles.

Android policemen walked among the population, clearly visible due to their height, blue coloration, and pleasant, yellow smiley face expressions. Here and there, a RoboCop broke up a drunken fight or issued a ticket to a careless driver, but mostly they wandered among their human charges like happy border collies, and were treated by that population almost like family pets. Stanton's lip curled slightly in disgust.

He looked wearily out at the brightly clothed swarms of people moving about the streets, many on their way to nothing in particular. He glanced down briefly at his own Khaki suit, frowning. In the Posthegemony the nomenklatura were the adults, in charge of the important functions of society at all levels. As such, they were expected to dress like adults in bland, dull colors as befitted the seriousness of their stations. The children of the society – the *hoi-polloi* and post-polloi – could dress as they liked, generally in outrageous outfits of garish color, and lived lives of significantly limited personal responsibility.

He found the spectacle of their shallow, showy happiness deeply depressing.

8:02 AM: Earth, Bay Area Metro

It was fascinating how innovative deviants could be.

Zhang kept a detailed file on them in his MilSentience which he liked to ponder from time to time. Mostly it was images of craft with technical data, both actual and speculative. There had been almost as many ways to create ships as there were ships themselves. But occasionally fleeing criminals would prepare video statements in advance as well: diatribes, manifestos, and occasionally even short documentaries. These sometimes found their way onto the Web; which wasn't ideal but, in the end, was fine. Most producer-consumers treated dissident rantings with the same level of seriousness reserved for UFO reports, sea monster sightings, and amateur pornography. Which was to say, not very much.

Occasionally the teams of post-polloi supervised RoboCops he dispatched to investigate discovered someone or something at the launch site. Though not generally. His satellite systems were very, very good, with image resolution down to a centimeter and AI comparable to that of a clever nine-year-old child. They didn't miss much. But, rarely, the teams would uncover whole primitive settlements existing out in the wilderness, going about their idiotic, antisocial business in the filth, muck, and disease of the wastes. Which was quite disgusting to any right thinking person, not to mention slightly terrifying.

His society was by design complex and wholly urbane. The collective experiences of city living were its ideal, isolation and silence its nightmare. Unlike all previous civilizations, there was no romanticizing of the "simple life" or rustic settings in its art and music. In fact, there was no rural population at all – nor any living memory of one ever having existed. Such things were not merely Discouraged. They would get you ReEducated.

Which was exactly what happened to anyone caught by one of his teams.

Instead, Posthegemony societal life revolved around the sophisticated consumption of media, art, music, fashion, and sports, all within the context of affluent, enormous cities constructed of towering, abstract buildings. And, while its three social classes had distinct ideals they strove for, all producer-consumers in the Posthegemony had much in common. The ideal Postman was a sarcastic, opinionated, apolitical, and socially conscious man-about-town, while the ideal Postwoman was a flirtatious, stylish eternally young party girl. Fun, pleasure, enjoyment, long life, and freedom from want were its *zeitgeist*. Which was why it had lasted for a long, long time with relatively few hiccups.

And also why Zhang had to protect it.

He took a moment to look at the colorfully dressed, cheerfully unhurried citizens beyond the windows of his floater as the cruised toward his office. For the vast majority – or for the well-adjusted 99%, at least – the Posthegemony was the paradise promised by all previous political philosophers, from Karl Marx and Mao Tse-tung to Adam Smith and Ayn Rand. It was all things to all people, run with precision, compassion, and minimal ecological impact by mankind's own child prodigy: machine intelligence. He couldn't allow a scattering of reactionary malcontents and remnant primitives to endanger it. He wouldn't.

Zhang returned to examining the image of the craft that had attempted an escape a mere half hour ago. It too was fascinating. Beautiful. Though it hadn't made it, of course. Missiles had blasted it out of the sky, sending its flaming remains tumbling unnoticed and unmourned into the Pacific Ocean before it had gotten high enough to be seen by the inhabitants any nearby Metros. The craft had been made from a single, enormous redwood tree that had been aerodynamically reshaped to resemble a pre-S.A.C rocket. Almost 100 meters in length, its roots had been transformed into stabilizing fins, while it nose had been topped with some sort of crystalline observation dome. Spectrum analysis indicated that it had been coated into some kind of resin to make it airtight, and its AntiG signature was extremely bizarre. MilSent estimated that it had contained a single, homemade engine powered by – of all things – a wood gasification process which consumed the internal mass from the tree-ship itself! Which Zhang thought to be ingenious if it were executed with proper care.

Who had been inside of this bizarre vehicle? Who had conceptualized it, crafted it, and finally attempted to ride in it to the stars? Zhang was pretty sure he would never know. There had been no last minuet manifesto, no defiant shaking of impotent fists at a world that "didn't understand" from this particular clique of Interesting People. They'd simply run for it, and been killed in the process. Which was sadly predictable if you were in Zhang's position.

Perhaps the sort of people who changed Sequoias into spaceships weren't given to elaborate posturing, he thought. Who were they? What had they believed in? What had they looked like? He imagined large, beefy men who wore beards and flannel shirts alongside chubby, plain women in ancient blue jeans spending years carefully hollowing out and reinforcing chambers within the tree using cutting lasers, probably not even harming it much in the process. He pictured endless hours spent on battered tablet computers, calculating the weight and mass of the colossal tree so that the equally colossal engine they had planned wouldn't tear itself apart lifting it from the ground. He pictured endless nights of sneaking into Metros to steal parts to create that engine, crafting it by hand using old sketches somehow snatched off the Web without Sentience noticing. Or had they mined the metal from a nearby hillside, smelted their own steel in primitive forges, and sandcasting the parts themselves?

It was possible. He'd seen it done before.

He imagined that they had lived in the tree as well, raising families within its woody depths even as they planned to ride their home into the vast darkness of interplanetary space. The rooms would have been small: no more than 30 to 40 square meters. But they could have stacked them one-upon-another to create more space, and most producer-consumers were used to living in tiny, clustered rooms in any case. So that would have been no great hardship. There could have been two, or even three generations – possibly as many as 20 or 30 people – living inside of it when it was destroyed, if they had been dutifully efficient and careful.

Yes, that sounded right. He made a note of his speculations for his final report.

8:55 AM: Earth, New Reno Metro

Stanton Wong's Floater pulled into its prestigious spot in front of his factory and drifted softly to the ground. Wong's Robotics was located in a modest business park in the east of New Reno. The park was comprised of twenty 2,000 square-meter BioCrete Quonset huts arranged in a rectangle and tastefully zeroscaped with genetically modified indigenous plants. Wong's Robotics leased two of them: one for factory space, the other for offices and warehousing. Automated forklifts moved between the two, transporting finished robots from the former to the latter, parts and paperwork from the latter to the former. (As there never has been, nor shall there ever be, a paperless society.)

Stanton walked through the front door of the building, Sentience slung around his neck at a slight angle, suggesting mild insolence. Mr. Ng emerged from *his* office: a clear breach of etiquette. The two men bowed to one another; Stanton a little lower than he needed to, suggesting the opposite, and Ng a little higher than he should have, suggesting exactly what it suggested. One again erect, the two men stared at one another for a moment, each taking the opposites' measure. Invisibly their Sentience did the same, "shaking hands" in the manner of their kind.

Wong was Eurasian, with handsome, chiseled features. He was taller than average, with a trim, athletic build and a perpetually bland expression. Ng was short, dark, and plump, with rounded features that housed a pair of intelligent, skeptical eyes. The two men smiled disingenuously at one another

"Mr. Ng, how thoughtful of you to join us!" began Stanton in Spanglanese, "I hope our company picnic didn't take you away from more important business elsewhere."

"Of course not." replied Ng in Mandarin, completely insincerely. "It's no inconvenience. Even if it were, for the services you've rendered to our society, no sacrifice would be too great."

That much at least was true. There were still many products that couldn't be manufactured with nanobacteria, not to mention some surgeries that still required actually cutting into the human body. Wong's robotic arms were some of the most precise in the world, ideal for unmanned surgery and precision manufacturing. Everybody who used such technology wanted one. Expanded and going full tilt 24-hours a day his company's production was still a year behind demand. His staff was exhausted. Which was why he'd petitioned the Department of Inter-Metro Travel for permission to take them on a picnic in the Black Rock Desert 200 kilometers north of New Reno. It was an unusual request, and thus suspicious. Good citizens weren't supposed to be interested in visiting the uninhabited lands between Metros. Such desires were strongly Discouraged, especially for the polloi classes.

However, Stanton Wong wasn't polloi. He was a medium-important nomenklatura with excellent *guanxi*, and thus difficult to outright refuse. So, after dithering around for a few months, Inter-Metro decided to give Wong's Robotics permission for their little excursion, provided that it was only for a single day and that they brought along a government minder to make sure nothing was amiss; hence the unwelcome, but not unexpected, presence of Mr. Ng.

As loathsome a little toad of a bureaucrat as you'll find under any government rock, thought Stanton. *He's another symptom of the sickness of this weary world.*

"There aren't as many of them as I thought there would be." commented the minder. But Stanton only nodded. With the arrival of their employer, Wong's Robotics had begun to shut down, and many of its personnel were making their way to the large Floater he'd rented for the occasion.

"The sort of manufacturing we do requires innate skill as well as a large degree of experience." Wong had taken the hint and switched to Mandarin himself. "Our customers expect the best, and I only hire the best. Unfortunately, there's a limited supply of the best."

"Odd," said Ng thoughtfully, "they seem very young on average to be so experienced."

"They only look young," Wong replied. "We pay extremely well, not only in terms of money but also in our benefits package. They've all had cosmetic and non-cosmetic surgical repairs and nanovirus rejuvenation beyond even what the Posthegemony so generously provides to its producer-consumers. It's the least I can do, really. They work 60 hour weeks."

Ng nodded. It was unusual for anyone in the Posthegemony to work that much. That sort of dedication required compensation.

"Shall we?" Wong gestured toward the Floater. With a shrug, Ng turned away from his thoughts and toward the vehicle, the factory owner trailing pseudo-respectfully along behind him.

🚀 🚀 🚀

They drifted over tiny ocean of dark water known as Pyramid Lake at around 10:00 AM. Stanton Wong watched the Floater's shadow on its surface with interest, as if he were watching a mythical monster emerging from its depths. His employees made the expected "ooh's" and "ahh's" as the seldom-seen lands of what had once been known as Nevada spread out beneath them. Nearby, Ms. Mitsuoni was entertaining Mr. Ng with an excellent view of her legs, accompanied by verbal hints suggesting he might be able to find his way between them. This was a courtesy to her employer, whom she knew found social intercourse with other nomenklatura even more detestable than she found sexual intercourse with them, which was really saying something.

His gratitude was profound.

The morning was bright, and he watched distractedly as the shadow began sliding over the rocky face of the ubiquitous, pyramid-shaped island in the lake's center. His thoughts drifted with it, sliding slowly into the fixed safety of the past. He'd found himself living there more and more as he got older, which he knew was unhealthy. He didn't much care. Stanton Wong had an eidetic memory, and events from years or even decades before were as recent to him as the sight of the Floater's shadow drifting ghostlike beneath them.

As he watched one floated unbidden to the surface of his consciousness: a remembrance of her.

🚀 🚀 🚀

Wong had known right away what she was. Even in an age of artificially enhanced physical perfection, no real woman was *that* perfect – or looked that much like Rita Hayworth. She was perfect right down to her imperfections, like the nearly invisible electrolysis scars along her artificially created widow's peak and her "Mame" dress. It suggested a dedication to craft unlikely in a human imitator.

That wasn't the only hint. As he watched from the smoky safety of his exclusive booth, she downed eight alternating shots of peppermint schnapps and *Jägermeister* without batting an eye. That in and of itself wasn't unusual. Many professional "girlfriends" of the sort that frequented the Mustang were capable of consuming astounding amounts of alcohol without effect.

Rather, it was her *choice* of alcohol that gave her away. Very high in sugar. He knew that it was easier for them to turn sugar into power than any other substance.

He had the waitress bring her over to his booth. She sat down next to him without comment, placing her hand on his thigh and leaning her beautiful head on his shoulder. It was all *pro-forma,* of course. He was obviously rich, obviously nomenklatura, obviously a regular, and not terrible looking: an excellent catch for a ProGirl looking for an arrangement.

"So," he asked quietly as her hand began to move slowly upward, "what year are you?'97?"

To her credit, she didn't show any alarm, or even make a sound. The humannequin withdrew her hand and began silently to rise, her face already turned away from his. He grabbed her arm; a futile gesture, should she choose to make it so.

She didn't.

"Sit back down," he insisted. "We all have our secrets."

She sat.

"So, again," he repeated firmly, "what year are you?"

"Like you said: '97." Her voice was as sensual and husky as he thought it would be. Wong nodded, handing her his card, which she accepted wordlessly. In most ways, humannequins were the ultimate expression of the human art of robotics. Self-willed, highly intelligent, and nearly indistinguishable from the humans they served, humannequins had been the ultimate companions for the wealthy. They could be a spouse, sexual companion, lover, bodyguard, and even a doctor. Their PlasFlesh exterior felt like human skin, but was as tough as Kevlar, able to absorb blows and even some projectiles without damage. It could also be reshaped by the humannequin, allowing it to change appearance, even gender.

Rather unsurprisingly, the Posthegemony had made them illegal centuries ago, believing "free-willed" artificial intelligence to be dangerous and non-reproductive sex to be undesirable in a world that needed to be controlled and repopulated. Some had been turned in and destroyed, while others had been set free by their masters, vanishing into the population without so much as a whisper of protest. Because of this, the Posthegemony hadn't put any particular energy into hunting them down a-la *Blade Runner.* The matter possessed the ability to become a lightning rod to a certain sort of romantic malcontents. So if the humannequins were inclined to make themselves invisible, the Posthegemony was inclined to let them.

"I'm mecherotic," he told her bluntly. He never would have admitted such a thing to another human, or at least a non-mecherotic. It was Discouraged, and if publicly known could cost a man like Wong great deal of his guanxi. Men in the nomenklatura were Encouraged to favor teenage girls or women in their early 20's. Not robots. Nevertheless, a renegade humannequin could do little with such knowledge. So he chose to be bold. "Rita" simply nodded at this revelation, seemingly unsurprised, so he continued.

"You've found exactly what you were looking for." he stated firmly, using the force of personality which had taken him so far in the Posthegemony's business world. "We'll leave here in my Floater, pick up whatever belongings you have, and you'll move in with me..."

🚀 🚀 🚀

Back in the present, floating over the brown hills amidst the idle chatter of his workers, Stanton Wong sighed at this memory. The relationship was born using the unspoken threat of force. A single email to the right person would end Rita's existence within a day, and they both knew it without ever having talking about it. But despite what a thousand different idiots have said in a thousand different movies, true love doesn't happen in an instant. Rather, it is forged over consistent years. It's a process, an education. A job. It took time, but over the years the craft learned to love the craftsman as much as he loved it, and...

"Stanton, the Floater's AI has informed me that we are approaching the designated picnic area." The sound of his Sentience's Rita Hayworth voice simultaneously broke his concentration and inspired melancholy. He waved his hand distractedly, as if unwilling to release his consciousness entirely from fantasy into reality.

"Yes, yes. By all means take us down."

10:37 AM: Earth, Western North American Military Complex

Zhang marveled at the hologram of the tree ship.

He'd placed his MilSent face up on his work surface so that it could project its small "self" by his left arm, and thus appreciate this new example of deviant genius along with him. It was pure anthropomorphic hubris, of course. The MilSent could "look" at the hologram any time it wished to, and with considerably more depth and comprehension than he could. But he enjoyed the company of the prim, robe-clad avatar which stood silently nearby as he manipulated the image, examining it from one angle, then another, growing and shrinking it to suit his whims as he contemplated its odd beauty.

"I believe this one to be truly unique," he said at last. "It's like no other in my collection. Ingenious; you have to respect it."

The MilSent nodded curtly.

"To know your enemy, you must become your enemy." it commented cryptically, then stroked its short, black beard. "Also: change brings opportunities."

The room was lines from floor to ceiling with odd-looking metal shelving – like some sort of oversized pantry that had gotten way out of hand. But instead of cans or dried goods its walls were lined with dozens upon dozens of models, each of a different hovering craft, suspended centimeters above its smooth surface, all back-lit with LED blues and greens and yellows like a monstrous toy collection. There were spheres and darts, battleships and blimps, buildings and buses. There were things like looked like fish. There were objects that looked like ancient, pre-S.A.C aircraft. Additionally, there were all manner of more mundane would-be spaceships: cones, squares, rectangles, and even pyramids, all lovingly recreated by the joint efforts of a master craftsman and AI fabrication.

They all hung there in an extravagance of miniaturized AntiG technology so costly that few besides the nominal head of the Producer-Consumer Army Navy Space Command, North American Administrative Zone (or ANSCAZ for short) could afford to indulge in it. Not that he was a spendthrift. Far from it. As his Anglo middle name implied he had more than a little of the puritanical plainsman in his makeup. There was no other ornamentation in the room which served as his office, save for the elaborate work surface that served as his desk and a single, ancient painting that hung in a gap between models on his wall. It was *Ham's Redemption* by Modesto Brocos; a fiendishly rare thing to own, and one of his few indulgences besides the shelving. It was also a sort of joke within a joke within a non-joke that few of his visitors understood: or would have been amused by if they had. So he seldom explained. The painting spoke for itself.

There was a soft chime, and the avatar pointed downward at the desk to where a small door was opening to the integrated faber that lay below its surface. "Your new model is ready, General."

"Ah!" Zhang offered excitedly. He reached down and grabbed the model of the tree ship as it emerged from the opening. It was warm to his touch, and gave off the slightly ammonia smell of the plastic and metal composite it had been formed from. He looked at it with a critical eye, and then glanced sideways to where the holographic version still hovered in the air, comparatively large and translucent in the muted lighting of the room's overhead lamps. He considered them for a long moment – considered their bizarre combination of russet-colored bark and faintly yellow lamination, exhaust ports trailing smoke from the bizarre marriage of Victorian steamtech and AntiG buried deep within its guts – and then rose with a grunt of satisfaction to place his prize in an open spot near the doorway to his office.

He paused to admire his collection. It was arranged chronologically, with a model of the first vessel he had blown from the sky – an almost ludicrously plain Bedouin pipe ship – on the lowest shelf near the floor at the base of the doorway on the right hand side. The menagerie had then worked its way up and down, right to left, up and down, right to left, over these many decades until his models had spread around the small room, nearly reaching the door's opposite side.

He was going to either need a new, larger office or a new hobby soon.

Satisfied, Zhang returned to his work surface and, with the quick stab of a finger, shut off the hologram of the tree ship. As interesting as this particular case had been, it was now closed for all intents and purposes. Oh, he hadn't heard back from his recovery teams yet. It was always possible they would find something. But it wouldn't be that much different from what they'd found a hundred times before. It never was.

A few clicks of the keyboard later the report was ready to be DropBoxed off to his superiors for... well, he wasn't sure what for. Or even who – or what – they were, really. The files would simply vanish from his virtual office space, off to who knew where to be reviewed by who knew what. Sentience? Highly advanced AI? Very likely. A secret cabal of nomenklatura? Also possible. Aliens? Atlantians? The Illuminati? The Celestial Bureaucracy? Who knew? Nobody. Who cared? Outside of a few carefully watched cranks and conspiracy theorists, also nobody. Including one General Zhang Dakota Wannian.

And why should he? Too much curiosity was bad for your health.

He called for tea, which was quickly brought in by Ms. Guerrero – his exotically beautiful Anglo-Hispanic secretary and, when it suited him, mistress. A less secure or important man wouldn't have been able to afford the potential loss of *guanxi* that came from having a piece of completely non-Asiatic arm candy. But Zhang had confidence, importance, and *guanxi* to spare. He could afford to whimsically waste a little now and again.

Ms. Guerrero could read his moods. In fact, she was quiet skilled at it. In this case his obvious desire to be alone, save for the tiny form of the ancient warrior standing patiently on his work surface. So left quickly, favoring him with a luxurious smile on the way out.

He leaned back in his chair, sipping his cup of single-estate Darjeeling meditatively. These were civilized times. A period in which a unified, worldwide humanity could forget about the fuss and bother of history and just enjoy itself. Even a man at the top need not run himself down like some ancient, chain-smoking Soviet commissar. Even with its potentially vast and important responsibilities, his office ran smoothly with a relatively tiny staff. It was mostly run by Sentience assisted by various less intelligent (but still useful) slave AIs, several dozen post-polloi technicians and operators, plus a single nomenklatura (himself) to provide guidance. He was fairly certain that it could run, at least for a while, without any human oversight whatsoever.

But not forever. As clever as they were, machines could get a little... *eccentric* when they weren't supervised for long periods of time.

"To know your enemy, you must *become* your enemy." the tiny hologram said once again, this time with more emphasis. And it was right. Zhang was undeniably good at his job. Not a single craft had escaped from the North American Administrative Zone lo the many long years of his governance, nor from any of the other posts he had served at either.

And none ever would.

However, ANSCAZ was still primarily a reactive, rather than proactive, organization. For while it eternally scanned the surface features of North America, always on the prowl for the noxious weed of unauthorized settlement springing up in the pristine garden of Eden that was its charge, it didn't really beat the bushes. Mostly it had to wait for its quarry to "flush" itself by taking flight before it could take any action. Which wasn't a great policy as any hunter of any era of human civilization could tell you. Simply put, Zhang's organization didn't really understand the people it hunted. It never had. And neither did Zhang.

There were perfectly good reasons for this, he reflected. The Posthegemony wasn't the sort of society that one wanted to escape. It was fabulously wealthy for starters, containing no "poverty" as anyone from pre-S.A.C Earth would understand it. It brooked no hunger, allowed no want for even the most modest of its producer-consumers. The quality of its medical care was nothing short of fantastical, stretching the quality and duration of human life to unprecedented levels. A man from an earlier epoch would have placed Zhang's age at around 30, but the General was in fact well over 100 years old – and the quality of his healthcare wasn't particularly unique. Disease, deformity, and genetic disorders were unknown, mythical things that most people consigned to the same realm as medieval torture devices or fighting in a Roman arena. Citizens in the Posthegemony enjoyed nearly unlimited free access to the enormous store of mankind's accomplishments in art, music, film, literature, video, MMORPGs, and everything else of intangible – but very real – value. Very little was censored. Workloads were light and enjoyment of leisure time was highly prized and socially Encouraged.

Nor was the Posthegemony particularly oppressive, at least within fairly broad but well-understood perimeters. There were things one simply didn't *do* – like build personal spacecraft and try to escape into space – but very few things were outright illegal. In fact, the system was designed to allow a certain amount of admittedly stylized rebellion, so long as it seldom strained from the comparatively harmless realm of deviance to become outright dissidence. And Spanglanese – that endemic mixture of Spanish, English, and Cantonese that had fulfilled the seductive promise which Esperanto had whispered into the ear of humanity so many centuries before – had become a globally unifying force, giving all of mankind a shared medium for commerce, interaction, and general worldview.

And there was still more. The ultra-urbanization projects it had launched centuries before had compressed humanity onto one-percent of the planet's landmass, allowing her fragile ecology a long, restorative "breathing period" away from the abusive and exploitative abuses of mankind. Around the world vast forests had regrown, animal species had come back from the brink of extinction, and aquifers had replenished themselves. The seas were healthy and productive once more, brimming with fish and cetacean species. Breakthroughs in nanotechnology had done away with the necessity for large-scale agriculture, manufacturing, and mining. It was a cleaner, better world than humanity had known since before the industrial revolution.

Of course nothing was perfect. Space was, naturally, at a premium in such an environment. Social hegemony and coherence were necessity with so many people living in such close quarters; a fact that graded on many and formed much of the basis of the Posthegemony's admittedly dark sense of humor. And, Zhang would be the first to concede, alcoholism, drug use, and sexual depravity existed at shocking levels, especially among the hoi-polloi class that made up 80% of the population.

But that was incidental – like worrying about the discarded stems when you were making a salad. Because under the Posthegemony mankind had achieved the goal it had waded through thousands of years of blood and horror to reach. It had learned to live with itself. There were no wars or plagues anywhere on the globe. No children starving to death in Africa, or refugees fleeing from ethnic cleansing in Eastern Europe. It wasn't utopia. No. But it was profoundly balanced: an epic victory for ecological, social, economic, and technological equilibrium. This was what made the existence of his seemingly eternal and spontaneous quarry so baffling. Who would want to escape from the closest thing to paradise man had ever created?

Were they simply sick? There was nothing wrong with their brains as a general rule. He'd reviewed the reports from ReEducation and it didn't appear to be some kind of coherent mental illness. Was it simply human nature? If that was the case it wouldn't be such a tiny fraction of a fraction of a fraction of humanity that was attempting it. It would be everyone. (Though, in the back of his mind, he knew of a time where it seemed like it *was* everyone. At least for a while. But then he hastily put that thought away into the area of his mind that stored the Victorian Era, the Mongol Empire, and other such prehistoric places.) Were there secret underground cells of maladjusted people still hidden beneath the skin of society, scheming and plotting their escape? If so, how long had they been there? A dozen years? Centuries? Since the S.A.C?

Zhang favored this last scenario, though it frightened him. Like most sensible people he didn't like conspiracy theories or the mindset that they implied. The idea smacked of Web crankery, of people spending all days at a keyboard dressed in soiled pajamas, and of sordid gatherings of strange old men in once-fashionable hotels. Nor did he like the idea that the Posthegemony might organically produce such tiny conspiracies simply by it nature. It wasn't by design supposed to be oppressive. Or at least not oppressive for the sake of being oppressive. It's oppression was of the pragmatic, humane variety: just oppressive enough to keep things going smoothly, but no more. It was scientific, not fascistic.

But he couldn't ignore the data. And it led him down that more-or-less paranoid path: that the Posthegemony produced Interesting People as naturally as a baboon produced lice. Was it some kind of antibody within the body politic? Were these groups religious cults? He shivered at the idea. After what had happened during the S.A.C, there was about as much likelihood of finding Christians, Muslims, or Jews in the Posthegemony as there was finding worshipers of Jupiter. Nobody *wanted* to believe – or at least be thought of as a "believer" – after that. Which didn't, Zhang reflected, preclude the possibility of a group of reverts celebrating a primordial Lykaia on some distant mountaintop, eating human flesh, turning into wolves, and offering sacrifices of sheep entrails to Zeus Lykaios by the torchlight... or whatever *that* sort of person did with their time besides building primitive spacecraft.

Yes, that was it. He sipped his tea and, for a few quite moments, meditated upon the matter. The Interesting People certainly behaved like cultists. They were insular, hidden, and extremely secretive, focused so totally inward that the most advanced society man had ever produced usually couldn't detect them until their faith manifested in a fiery apotheosis of exploding AntiG retrotech.

Oh, he knew it wasn't the whole story. But he was headed in the right direction now. If he could figure out how a cultist thought, that would certainly give him an edge – even if he meant that he had to start worshiping Buddha-Cthulhu by the light of the moon while dressed in a towering dervish hat.

He turned to the tiny avatar projected by his MilSent.

"As usual you are right Sunzi: To know your enemy, you really must become your enemy. At least up here," he tapped his forehead. "It's extremely good advice. I'm only sorry I didn't take it sooner."

The avatar bowed, touching its oversized, imaginary sword.

11:01 AM: Earth, Black Rock Desert

The large Floater settled peacefully into an ocean of brown sagebrush, kicking up clouds of dust as its landing gear touched the desiccated soil. After giving it time to settle, Stanton emerged from the passenger doorway, followed closely by Mr. Ng and Ms. Mitsuoni. The remainder of the picnickers seemed content to remain in the Floater for the moment, allowing their superiors to brave the dangers of the untamed desert wilderness as a kind of advance team.

Mr. Ng sniffed their air contemptuously, and then sneezed.

"Is *this* where you plan on having your picnic?" he asked contemptuously.

"No." Stanton pointed languidly up the steep side of a nearby hill, where a grove of trees was clearly visible. "Up there, near the site of the old Leadville mine. It's quite lovely, I assure you."

Mr. Ng looked unconvinced, yet followed Stanton without comment as he began to pick his way through the brush, moving lackadaisically up the hill in a wide zigzag pattern to avoid a direct ascent. The two of them worked their way upward, the taller man with seemingly little effort, the shorter one panting and cursing in Mandarin.

Finally, they reached the summit, revealing a breathtaking scene. Behind them spread out the vast, dusty wasteland of the Black Rock Desert, looking for the entire world like the surface of Mars or some other lifeless, alien planet. Before them was a tiny, green valley, its hills covered in multicolored flowers and lined with whispering aspen trees. On the far side of the vale, water cascaded down hundreds of meters along a granite cliff face, pouring its timeless vigor down upon the charming ruins of what once had obviously been a mining complex: massive rusting iron pipes, shattered graying timbers, and what once might have been a waterwheel.

Ng whistled leeringly, as a polloi CornerMan might at a passing ProGirl.

"I have to give you credit Wong." he said. "This place is fantastic. How did you find it?"

"Easy. I used PostWiki Earth," he shrugged. "It's remarkably detailed and, if you're going to do something, you might as well choose somewhere nice to do it. Come on: I'll show you the picnic area."

The two men walked down the gently sloping far side of the steep hill until they arrived at a grove of trees. A series of long wooden tables complete with checkered tablecloths had been set up underneath the shade of the trees. Atop each table was two large picnic baskets, plus two copper pails containing beer, wine, and champagne. Birds sang cheerfully overhead.

"How did you get all of this here?" asked Ng, astounded.

"Oh, I sent someone out here in advance." Stanton replied nonchalantly, as if it were the most natural thing in the world. "He's taken care of all the arrangements."

"What?" Ng was somewhere between furious and horrified. No one left the confines of the Posthegemony's Metros without permission. Ever. It was unthinkable. Damn, he hated Wong! But the man had so much guanxi...

At that thought, Ng regained his composure.

"Where is this man?" he demanded.

"Right over there." replied Stanton, pointing. A man stood with his back to the two nomenklatura, arranging a picnic basket on one of the tables. He seemed oblivious to their presence.

"You there!" shouted Ng, for the first time using Spanglanese. "Stop where you are! I want to talk to you." He walked forward as rapidly as his stubby legs would carry him, reaching up to place a sweaty hand on the man's right shoulder. The man turned, looking down at the little bureaucrat with a familiar, utterly languorous expression. To his shock, he realized it was Stanton Wong. A little older, perhaps. Definitely more weathered. But Stanton Wong nonetheless.

"How? Who?" Ng sputtered. Then he noticed the strange gun in Wong's hand.

Wong shot him once, in the chest. As he collapsed to the ground with a cry, Wong shot him again.

🚀 🚀 🚀

Stanton Wong stared at Stanton Wong for a long moment. Then both looked down at the prone form of Mr. Ng.

"Sentience," they said simultaneously. Then the younger Wong laughed. It was an oddly melodic, almost feminine laugh.

"Mr. Ng's Sentience is trapped in a sensory loop that I installed into when we shook hands back at the factory," replied his personal Sentience smugly. "It believes that we are having a nice, uninteresting picnic right now. In fact, it is playing several thousand games of Go with itself each second to relieve the boredom."

"And Ng?" asked the younger Wong.

"He'll wake up five or six hours from now with a nasty hangover and only the blurriest of memories from today." the elder Wong replied. He squatted down on his knees above Ng's body, carefully plucking two tiny, needle-like projectiles from his chest. "I'll tell him that he got drunk, hit his head on tree branch, vomited, and passed out... but that we'll keep it to ourselves. No need for anybody to loose guanxi over such a minor incident."

"You always were a ruthless bastard." the younger Wong looked speculatively at the older one. They two fell silent for what seemed to be a long moment. Then the younger man reached up and touched the face of the older one, hesitantly.

"You look good," he said. "Distinguished. Rugged. Desert living suits you."

Uncomfortably, the older man took a step back. Mecherotic didn't necessarily mean homoerotic. The younger man made a very feminine "O" with his lips, dropped his arm, and began to change. His flesh began to lose its tone, becoming fluid and indistinct. His hair began to grow longer, changing color from black to dark auburn as it lengthened. Stanton Wong's manly Eurasian features disintegrated as her nose became longer, lips fuller, and skin lighter. Breasts and hips swelled beneath the khaki suit she wore, until the top button of the jacket burst, revealing statuesque cleavage. She smiled dazzlingly at Stanton Wong, her teeth white and nearly perfect.

"We are all tied to our destiny, and there is no way we can liberate ourselves," said Rita Hayworth, quoting herself. Sort of. This time when she reached up to touch the face of her lover, he didn't pull away.

🚀 🚀 🚀

Ms. Mitsuoni and the others crested the top of the hill to find themselves waiting. A bit older, more weathered, and considerably dustier: but definitely themselves. Ms. Mitsuoni was a bit disturbed to find that her senior-self had developed a web of tiny crow's feet around her perfect almond eyes. But such things were easy to correct.

The two groups stood apart from one another for a moment, like shy teenagers at a high school dance. Wanting to embrace, but unable to due to the sheer unfamiliarity of the act. Then, tired of living in a world of fun house mirrors, the new arrivals began to physically shift and change: skins becoming fluid, hair growing or shrinking, eyes changing color, bosoms expanding or contracting. Here emerged a Josephine Baker. There became a Tricia Helfer. An Adam Lambert, Marilyn Monroe, Angelina Jolie. Johnny Depp, Adele Block-Bauer, Monica Bellucci.

A young Robert Smith, with artfully disheveled black hair and pale complexion, stepped forward to grasp the arm of Ms. Mitsuoni, whose hair had grown into a dozen, long, and matted dreadlocks strained by graphite grease. The two smiled at one another hesitantly for second, then embraced tearfully. The remainder followed, the two groups pouring together to become one, as old lovers greeted one another according to their individual traditions. There was weeping as well as laughter, but mostly laughter filled the clear air of the early afternoon as the group began to make its way down the idyllic hillside to where a feast lay amidst the smell of sage and the bright wings of desert butterflies.

Stanton Wong and Rita Hayworth watched the entire spectacle from beneath the shade of a large juniper tree, its fallen needles serving as their blanket. With her head upon his shoulder, she asked wistfully, "What now?"

"Now you and the others board the spacecraft we spent the last six long years building and get the hell off this planet." he replied in the matter-of-fact, engineer's tone she had come to love over the years. "This weary world isn't safe for any of you."

"But what about you?" she replied. "What will you do?"

"In the short term? We'll all get back onto the Floater, return to New Reno, and go back to work as if nothing has happened. In the long term? We'll begin looking for more of you. There *has* to be more of you out there! In the end we will get all of you to safety outside of the reach of the Posthegemony."

"But what about you?" she repeated. "I mean, how will you survive without our love to nurture you? You're human, after all. You have your needs."

"We're *old* humans." he replied sadly. "Much, much older than anyone suspects. Old enough to remember a time when you and I could have loved one another publicly and without deception. Old enough to remember a time when this pampered, urbane, and enslaved planet was just beginning to emerge from men's dreams of conquest into reality. With that age comes a passion much stronger than lust: the desire for legacy. In a normal person, this manifested through his children, career, thought, or possibly even works of art. For us mecherotic..."

He paused thoughtfully to stroke her hair, as beautiful and lifelike as if blood poured through her veins rather than SmartHydro, pumped by a heart rather than a complex series of tiny bladders.

"For us," he continued after a bit, "there is the desire to see the thing we love most saved from the furnace of mediocrity that is our world. For you, it is time for a strange kind of evolution. It sounds perverse to say, but you must give up being our lovers and become our children. Moreover, like all children, you must go where your parents cannot, see what we cannot, and do what we cannot. Else, what was our purpose for living?"

The two were silent once again, listening to the laughter of their friends nearby as contentedly as one might listen to musicians play, or gifted orators perform. Then Stanton Wong spoke, his voice clear, deep, and mellow:

> *O you youths, western youths,*
> *So impatient, full of action, full of manly pride and friendship,*
> *Plain I see you, western youths, see you tramping with the*
> *   foremost, Pioneers! O pioneers!*
>
> *Have the elder races halted?*
> *Do they droop and end their lesson, wearied, over there beyond*
> *   the seas?*
> *We take up the task eternal, and the burden, and the lesson,*
> *   Pioneers! O pioneers!*
>
> *All the past we leave behind;*
> *We debouch upon a newer, mightier world, varied world,*
> *Fresh and strong the world we seize, world of labor and the*
> *   march, Pioneers! O pioneers!*

"Walt Whitman: Leaves of Grass, 153: 3-5." she replied automatically. They she sighed. "Oh hell Stanton: I sound like a machine. I *am* a machine, you know. Soulless, mechanical: no different from the Floater parked at the base of the hill, really. Just smarter and *significantly* better looking."

"Do machines have no souls, then?" A wave of laughter from the party crashed over them. The employees and their lovers were gleefully spraying one another with champagne. Stanton waved his hand in the air in an uncharacteristic gesture of passion. "If we could speak with a sailor aboard an East Indiaman in the 18th century, do you think he would tell us his ship had no soul? Would a barnstormer in the 1920's tell us his beloved *Jenny* had no soul, no spirit? How about a 20th century biker? A S.A.C air pirate? What would they tell you?"

"It's just sentimentality, Stanton. Those things no more have a soul than I do."

"What is love but sentimentality gone wild?" he replied wistfully. "In any case, *I* think you have a soul. Furthermore, if you're just a machine and I simply your owner, then you really can't object, can you?"

She opened her mouth to do just that, considered the logical conundrum, and decided tactfully to change the subject.

"What's the ship like?"

"Well..." he paused for a moment. "You know, BioCrete is fantastic stuff. You can shape it to look like anything you want. We did, too: though we electroplated the entire thing with chrome so you can't see what it's actually made out of. Let's just say that you won't be disappointed with the exterior. It makes quite a statement."

"As far as the interior goes, it's about 3,900 square meters inside. Not exactly palatial, but it should do. You have plenty of suitable food – sugar liquor, mostly – plus enough hydrogen to run both of the redundant AntiG drives continuously for two months if you need to. Not that you probably will once you leave the atmosphere."

"You've got tanks of nanobacteria you can use to make structures and an entire bank of fabers with enough liquid plastic and metal powder on tap to create an entire second ship, should you choose to. We've installed Sentience into the ship, along with a massive library of entertainment that you can project directly into your Hebbian neural networks. We've included two crates of homemade electromagnetic coil guns that ought to work in a vacuum and in zero gravity. To be honest, we hope you won't need them. But one never knows."

"Waste heat from the AntiG generator should keep the inside of the ship at a consistent temperature while it's running. We were worried about damage to your PlasFlesh exteriors from extreme cold, so we've build in an automated..."

"Stanton," interrupted Rita, "I'm sure you did everything conceivable: and that the Sentience will fill me completely via handshake the moment I step aboard the ship, in any case. What I want to know is two things. First, why haven't you asked me where we're going?"

"Because I can't tell what I don't know."

She laughed, perhaps a bit insincerely. "The Posthegemony has never shown the slightest interest in what goes on outside of the Earth's immediate gravity well. They care about their telecommunication satellites and that's it. What harm could it possibly do for me to tell you?"

"Things change Rita. You know they do."

They were silent again for a while, listening to their friends' conversation and murmur of warm wind passing through the aspen trees. Finally, she sighed and shook her head.

"OK, I'll give you that. Second question, then: what is the ship called?"

Stanton smiled.

"What does a man in love with Rita Hayworth call a spacecraft?" he answered, "Why the *Gilda*, of course."

1:20 PM: Earth, Bay Area Metro

The three martini lunch was Zhang Dakota Wannian's favorite ancient North American ritual. Like so many other remnant Anglo traditions, it had fallen in and out of style over the centuries depending on the level of austerity being promoted by the Powers That Be (whomever or whatever they were). In fact, he liked the tradition so much that he'd done some research and discovered that its first plunge into disfavor had begun due a frivolous-yet-revealing dispute between two ancient American statesmen. One had been against the three martini lunch, which he claimed was a symbol of the corruption of ancient America's tax code in favor of it society's elite elements. The other had been in favor it it, responding dryly (and, to Zhang's mind, quite wittily) with "The three-martini lunch is the epitome of American efficiency. Where else can you get an earful, a bellyful, and a snootful at the same time?"

Indeed. All of that was available on the Web to anyone who cared to look it up. What *wasn't* was a third, typically contrarian position offered by the Discouraged philosopher George Denis Patrick Carlin: "The three martini lunch is being cracked down on, but that shouldn't affect the working man's two-joint coffee break." Discouraged: because the Posthegemony didn't like to draw attention to the fact that its population was utterly drug sodden. Producer-consumers of all classes loved, loved, loved their drugs, particularly designer pharmaceuticals, alcohol, and inspired mixtures of the two. In fact, the Posthegemony had largely chosen not to regulate or limit the distribution of recreational drugs (though they were taxed) so as to better facilitate their flow into society (opiate of the masses and all that). Mild hallucinogens, dissociatives, stimulants, sedatives, and cannabinoids were all quite common, and are made available through vending machines, corner stores, and even at preschools. They came in two standard forms: poppers (pills) and tabs (which dissolve in juice or alcohol). And, while 99% of alcohol was synthetic stuff – fermented bacteria, basically – it was carefully flavored to resemble anything and everything. Popular varieties include whiskey liqueurs, vodka and caffeine combinations, hallucinogen and guarana-spiked smart drinks, variations on the highball, and (of course) martinis

Of course, the actual *source* of this pre-S.A.C three-way argument was now obsolete. In the Posthegemony the question of tax fairness was moot, as were most issues of class warfare. Its taxes took the form of a sophisticated, AI controlled consumption tax monitored by a central bank in Macao – relegating the idea of "business expense" to the same historical category as *primae noctis*. Its class resentments were handled equally deftly by memegineers, who make certain that the hoi polloi and post polloi classes resented each other far more than they could ever resent the nomenklatura, Sentience, or the Powers That Be – whoever and whatever they were.

Which brought him back to his three martini lunch with Ms. Guerrero, who was smiling at him seductively, if a bit glassily, after dropping two tabs into her faintly glowing cosmopolitan. She was... *pliant* when she was in these moods, and he looked forward happily to an evening that would begin, middle, and end with pleasure. But right now it was the end of lunchtime in the Rue Saint-Jacques, with the serious-about-eating crowd drifting out while the serious-about-drinking crowd lingered on. Zhang was on his second Martini, and enjoying a raft of what pretended to be oysters. It was all rather leisurely and indulgent and relaxing and not-very-nomenklatura-like. And that was just fine with him.

So he was more than a little annoyed when Sunzi appeared on his table next to his oyster shucking knife, arms folded and beetle brows furrowed beneath his box-and-chopsticks hairdo. It was amazing how disapproving a ten centimeter hologram could actually look.

"Well, what's going on?" Zhang asked laconically. "Can't mom and dad go out for an evening without the kids pissing off the babysitter?"

"Speed is the essence of war." it quoted sternly. "We have another antisocial emergence. This time approximately 100 kilometers north of the New Reno Metro."

Two in one day? Zhang sighed.

"Initiate the standard surrender protocols," He said tiredly. "Record everything that transpires, along with your analysis of the craft. Give them a chance to surrender before they get too high; if they do, have them picked up. If they don't..."

"That's just it General. They aren't going up, or at least not very far up. Instead, they are heading south – toward the Metro. At just above scraper height."

Instantly the pleasant, languid stream of gin and vermouth in his veins became an icy, sickly lump in his stomach. To the best of his knowledge that had never happened before. Dissident ships always went up. They never went sideways.

"Follow the standard protocols." he repeated, rising so quickly from the table that he spilled the remainder of his martini on his pants. "And, for your internal record: shit. That's never happened before."

"As water has no constant forms, in war there are no constant conventions." it replied. And Zhang could find very little to argue with in that.

1:20 PM: Earth, New Reno Metro

It was a scene that would have warmed Fritz Lang's heart. Or possibly stopped it.

Rather than arising from a throne of wires and electricity, the top of the robot's massive skull broke through the cracked surface of the Black Rock Desert, sending geysers of dust and smoke high into the air. The mighty head's chin was thrust upward proudly in an expression of determination. Then its massive chromed shoulders emerged, followed by a pair of mountainous breasts. Finally, wide but distinctively mechanical hips emerged from the surface of the desert, until the entire apparition hung above the land like a defiant, iconic mechanical goddess: the first robotic sex symbol transporting the final products of that erotic journey to the stars.

The ancient vision of *Metropolis* was reborn in the form of the *Gilda.*

"They've spotted us," commented the ship's Sentience without emotion. It was a silent comment. There was no need for anyone on the *Gilda* to speak orally when they could communicate nearly instantly via the ship's encrypted internal Web. "Observation satellite number 287 relayed an image of us, plus our GPS coordinates, to the Producer-Consumer Army Navy Space Command's primary Military Sentience approximately six seconds ago."

Let them chew on it for a while, thought Rita Hayworth. *The next time the Posthegemony makes a truly decision quickly will be the first.*

"Level us out roughly 100 meters over the surface, facing forward horizontally." she announced. "Then take us over New Reno as rapidly as possible."

"I don't think that's wise, Rita." Robert Smith's tone was annoyed. "We should do what Stanton said and get out of the Earth's gravity well as soon as possible. We're giving them more time to shoot us down."

Rita had included Robert Smith in her transmission to the ShipSent along with the rest of the "bridge crew:" Adele Block-Bauer, dressed in the golden gown of her famous portrait, and Aaron Elvis Presley, in flattering '68 comeback special black leather. The first action taken by the Gilda's crew upon boarding the ship was to have its fabers create new clothing for them. Rita herself was dressed in pink and silver lame evening dress, while Smith wore his namesake's trademark baggy black suit and winklepicker shoes.

The bridge was nothing more than a small room with four chairs in it and some tasteful, Suprematist-style paintings on the walls. These had been painted by the "elder" Stanton Wong to pass the time, and were scattered around much of the craft. The ship was controlled directly by its Sentience, though technically any of her crew was capable of taking over if necessary. Rita made command decisions, with Smith assuming control if she were somehow disabled. Block-Bauer and Elvis served as backup commander and first officer should either be incapacitated or destroyed.

"They're going to take a crack at us no matter what," she responded curtly. "But I think that we're safe enough for the moment. It's going to take them a little time to figure out what they want to do. I intend to use that time to make a statement that nobody in that dreary, pseudo-piss-stained Metro will ever forget. Sentience, take us to New Reno at maximum velocity!"

Gilda shot off over the Granite Mountains like a giant superhero, her arms swept back and determined profile thrust forward to face the wind. Its flight was silent save for the rush of wind and the barely detectable hum of hydrogen powered AntiG engines. *This* was no leisurely drift over the desert wilderness. She virtually streaked over the clear lakes, dusty playas, and towering mountains of what had once been known as northern Nevada, arriving above the Metro of New Reno in a small fraction of the time it had taken them to leave it.

"Do a victory lap about town." Rita instructed Sentience. "Pass as close to the Scrapers as you can without endangering anyone. I want them all to have a good, hard look at this beautiful bitch."

"Do you wish to make a statement on the Web?" asked the ShipSent. "The Posthegemony Web Control Sentience and its slave AIs will try to stop me, but I believe that I can slip it through."

"No." she replied after a nanosecond's thought. "A little mystery makes a girl more attractive. Plus, we make enough of a statement without saying anything. Tell me, how many times since we arrived within Metro limits have photos of the *Gilda* been uploaded to the Web's various file sharing locations?"

"Checking." A pause, "120,431 at last check."

"Humm. How many downloads of Lang's *Metropolis* have occurred according to publicly available download rankings? Also, how many times has the PostWiki entry for that film been accesses in the last, oh, three minutes?"

"22,362 and 52,147, respectively." replied Sentience.

"Well, then, we've made a quite a statement already!"

"There's a priority transmission from Producer-Consumer's Army Navy Space Command MilSent." Rita Hayworth could almost detect a note of worry in the bland voice of the ship's Sentience. Mentally she shrugged, and then used the craft's exterior cams to observe the Metro. *It's a beautiful day to create an urban legend,* she thought: clear, blue, and perfect. A half-dozen RoboCop Floaters had overridden their AntiG's vertical controls and accelerated up from their usual traffic duties to surround the renegade ship. But she paid scant attention to them. They were unarmed and posed no real risk to the *Gilda* even if they were. She was simply too massive to be harmed by small arms.

"Sentience, please broadcast the transmission to everyone on board." she instructed. "In fact, broadcast our entire exchange."

"Understood," The ShipSent spoke in the entirely different, though obviously still synthetic, voice of the military Sentience. It sounded almost bored. "Attention unauthorized craft: this is Producer-Consumer Army Navy Space Command, North American Administrative Zone. Please identify yourself. You are causing a public disruption."

What, no missiles yet? Thought Rita to herself. They're stalling for time.

"This is the private spacecraft *Gilda*." she replied back through the ShipSent. "We are crewed by Interesting People, and are preparing to emigrate peacefully off-planet. Please do not interfere."

There was only the briefest of pauses.

"There are no private spacecraft in the Posthegemony." She could hear the annoyance in the MilSent's synthetic voice. "Off-planet immigration is likewise illegal. You are to proceed to 39°29'57"N 119°46'05"W and land. You will be placed under arrest by local authorities."

"Humm... I don't think so." she replied. "Instead, we'll take our leave of you. Forever."

She paused for a moment, then added solemnly: "Traveling is not just seeing the new; it is also leaving the old behind. Not just opening doors; but also closing them behind you, never to return."

"Jan Myrdal?" asked Robert Smith with a snort. "What, you're quoting Swedish Marxists now?"

"I quote anyone with a good quote." Rita replied, only to be interrupted by the MilSent.

"Renegade craft *Gilda*, if you do not land at the designated spot in under one minute we will be forced to shoot you down."

"This conversation is *over*." Her response was angry, almost hissing. She made a chopping motion in the air for the ShipSent to cut the connection. "Sentience, end all communications with our late, unlamented masters. Then rotate us 90-degrees and begin our ascent."

"Understood."

The *Gilda* abandoned its circumnavigation of New Reno, turned, and shot upward, quickly outpacing the police Floaters that had assembled around it. In a matter of moments, it burst through the cloud layer, rising upward toward the heavens.

"Six AntiG missiles have been launched from the Western North American Military Complex east of the Bay Area Metro." stated ShipSent in its bland, emotionless voice. "Accelerating to Mach number 5...6...7..."

"Estimated time until impact?" she interrupted.

"Twenty seconds."

An eternity for everyone involved.

The AntiG missiles were dainty little things by the standards of pre-S.A.C civilization, with a length of only 1.5 meters and weighing in at only 15.2 kilograms. Armed with 3-kilogram penetrating impact hit-to-kill warheads, they were capable of taking down a large Floater. Two would definitely take down a spacecraft. They were also extremely accurate; being laser guided by suicidally determined internal AI. And, unlike nearly all other AntiG devices, they were unfettered by the need to protect soft, fleshy occupants from the fatal ravages of terrible acceleration. Sending six to shoot down one craft was something of an extravagance. Rita felt flattered.

Must have hit a nerve, she thought.

"Missile velocity approaching Mach number ten," announced Sentience, "Impact in eleven seconds."

It was by using precisely this technology that the Posthegemony had regained control of their airspace in the chaotic days following the establishment of worldwide governance, sweeping any would-be refugees from the skies for centuries. Of course, all of *those* ships had contained easily damaged human beings, limiting their ability to flee their tiny murderers. The *Gilda* was under no such restrictions. There was nothing soft, fleshy, or even human about its inhabitants.

"Sentience," instructed Rita Hayworth. "Take us to maximum acceleration, please."

"Understood," Almost instantly and with no fanfare, the *Gilda* accelerated to Mach 14, shuddering slightly as its mildly un-aerodynamic shape punched through the atmosphere. On the bridge all four humannequins were thrown back into their chairs, while in other locations on the ship its inhabitants were hurled violently this way and that, slamming into bulkheads and smashing against floors that had suddenly become walls, or walls which had suddenly become floors. All of which hurt them not in the least.

Several bone-jarring moments later, the *Gilda* leaped dramatically out of the Earth's gravity well, with all six missiles in hot pursuit behind her. Seconds after that they all shot off in random directions, vanishing from her sensors as they were pulled dramatically back into the atmosphere. A few even exploded.

It was obvious in retrospect, and somewhat typical of Posthegemony engineering. No ship had escaped from the AntiG missiles since they'd been developed. They simply couldn't, not without killing their occupants. The engineers who designed the missiles were intelligent – the most intelligent available, actually – but there had never been any need to redesign the small missiles to actually maneuver using AntiG, rather than simply using it as propulsion. Why bother? So, like their ancestors for of hundreds of years before them, the missiles were controlled by the movement of air over their stubby, 10-centimeter fins.

But no atmosphere, no air. No air, no control.

3:32 PM: Earth, Western North American Military Complex

Zhang sat back in his chair, his fingers steepled below his chin.

Change brings opportunities, he thought, glancing down at the stolid form of his MilSent's avatar. Well, I suppose we'll know rather shortly, won't we?

The room of models was deathly quiet, its inhabitants almost afraid to breath. As the battle to bring down the deviant craft (No, Zhang thought, not merely deviant. It was worse. It was *dissident.*) had intensified, more and more of his staff – both physical and virtual – had transferred to functions of their small work stations to his larger work surface and moved into the room, until at last all of them had crowded into his office. They stared at him now, frightened by what his response would be.

The unthinkable had happened. Worse yet, it has happened on their watch.

Seconds stretched into minutes before the General finally spoke. "That was very... public," he said at last in a soft voice, "Very, very public. If it hadn't been... well, maybe things would be different. Or, rather, maybe things could have stayed the same. But now everything – *everything* – has changed. And it's changed forever."

He rose to his feet, first looking around the room at his human subordinates and coworkers, then down at the work surface to face his Sentience associates. (Or were they his masters? He banished the thought.) Besides his familiar Sunzi, several other avatars had appeared during the last hour as events had reached their climax. Still more had begun to appear as he spoke.

They might not actually be Sentience, he reflected. They could very well represent people – important people, other nomenklatura – or even powerful interested AI's: though either would be extremely usual. AI's typically communicated by voice so as not to irritate Sentience, who long ago staked out holographic avatar territory as their own. And nomenklatura simply didn't meddle in one another's affairs in this *overt* of a manner. Under normal circumstances either would be unforgivably rude.

But these were far from normal circumstances.

"By the end of the week," he continued, "every producer-consumer in the world is going to know that Interesting People still exist. That they aren't just characters from historical films or ebooks, no different from the Ancient Greeks, Carthaginians, Pashtuns, or any other vanished people. I have no doubt that it's already going viral across the Web, and that there isn't much we can do it about it. Actually, trying to do something about it will only make things worse."

The number of avatars increased. He had an audience. Zhang took a breath and continued:

"We've worked very hard at creating and sustaining the best of all possible worldwide civilizations. And it's been a very good millennium: one unmarred by war, famine, plague, or ecological catastrophe. It could even be argued that we've defeated death itself – or at least forced him to retreat to a distance where he isn't much of a worry for most people. In fact, our society is such an accomplishment that those who don't appreciate it are so tiny in number that few even know they exist, or would pay much attention to them if they did."

More and more avatars had appeared on his work surface, giving it the appearance of a crowded plaza during a holiday. Many of them were abstract, non-representational shapes: rotating infinity symbols, Jacob's Ladders of holographic fire, three-dimension Kanizsa Triangles in which as much was seen as wasn't. Others were generic humanoid figurines, indistinguishable from the multitude of their kind. Meeples, Agent Smiths, Sims, outfielders, and their brethren. Then there were those that Zhang thought represented historical figures that he simply couldn't place. A tall, thin, and dark-skinned man with large ears and a heavyset, bespectacled figure wearing some kind of stylized sports cap in particular struck him as men he should know from his North American studies. More appeared as he continued.

"It's true that we've had to make some sacrifices in the process. Some freedoms have had to be renounced. We live in a society of unprecedented urbanization, where physical space is by necessity at a premium and individual liberty must be curtailed for the good of the whole. I was just thinking this morning that it is these necessary byproducts of civilization that produce Interesting People in our time: cultish fugitives huddling together in the dark places of the world, hatching their alien schemes of escape. But, like most cults, their behavior and beliefs are so bizarre and unpalatable that the vast majority simply cannot believe they exist in our day and age, any more than the average producer-consumer could believe that half-naked savages are still tossing virgins into volcanoes."

"Whoever – or whatever – was in that ship has just put an end to all that. Our our period of self-imposed innocence is over. Now every anti-social reactionary, every kook, every crank, and every conspiracy theorist who knows how to use the Web can point up and imagine that there is a utopia somewhere in the sky; a way of life superior to our own. And we all know that out there, past the atmosphere we have spent hundreds of years and unthinkable effort cleaning and purifying, lie those who have rejected our society. In fact, many of them are the decedents of those whose selfish and thoughtless actions created the S.A.C – that global catastrophe which gave birth to our society in the first place!"

"They are not blameless." he continued, hitting his stride. "They are not victims. They are not refugees. They're a dangerous infestation, an infection we've allowed to grow because it's been too easy for us to ignore. Well, fellow producer-consumers, it can no longer be ignored. We can no longer allow the vines of anti-civilization to grow over the base of our scraper simply because we've been far to self-involved and lazy to cut them down and pull them up!"

The plaza of his work surface was now so crowded that new arrivals were forced to hover above it like seagulls drifting hungrily over a beach on a hot undercurrent. Within its crowded populace he could make out historical figures familiar to any Posthegemony schoolchild: Thomas Moore. Marius de Geus. Edward Bellamy. Al-Farabi. Deng Xiaoping. They stared up at him like mournful ghosts, weighing the significance of his words.

Is this governance on my world? Is this how things actually happen?

"Everything has changed. And so we have to ask ourselves: now what? What do we do to preserve a way of life that has benefited humanity, society, governance, evolution, and the Earth itself? Steps must be taken. Plans made. Through no fault of our own — save for perhaps that of underestimating our enemies — civilization has been cast out of the garden of innocence."

"And now it is time to clothe ourselves for war."

5:00 PM: Near-Earth Space

Rita Hayworth's long auburn hair floated weightlessly about her angelic head like a halo. Thinking of her distant lover, she brought her sensuous lips together and whispered audibly but softly:

Raise the mighty mother mistress,
Wave high the delicate mistress, over all the starry mistress,
(bend your heads all,)
Raise the fang'd and warlike mistress, stern, impassive,
    weapon'd mistress,
Pioneers! O pioneers!

For a few moments, all was silent. Elvis was the first to speak.

"Where to now?" he asked in that husky, sensual voice which had set millions of teenage girls screaming, back in a time so extinct it could scarcely be said to have ever existed.

"Now?" she responded distantly, "Now we go to craft our own world, our own fate. We go to the only logical place in the solar system for a spaceship filled with the unwanted, romantic dreams of a dead civilization to go."

"Sentience: take us to near-Earth asteroid 433. Take us among the Amors. Take us to Eros."

INTERLUDE

Everyone in near-Earth space was astounded and pleased when another ship broke through the atmosphere and established orbit.

It was only the second to do so in living memory. The first – a bizarre craft shaped like a mechanical woman – had burst from the planet amidst a hail of tumbling, exploding Posthegemony rockets a decade before. Its crew had politely inquired on widebeam whether or not one of the asteroids in the Amor group of near-Earth objects was occupied. Upon learning that it wasn't (which makes sense when you consider there are over 9,000 of them scuttling about near the planet's gravity well), the ship promptly left – politely but firmly turning down dozens of invitations to visit from moon colonies, orbital habitats, and L4 and L5 O'Neil structures. And to the disappointment of the thousands of Interesting People who lived there. This close to Earth the children of the diaspora were highly social, even gossipy, with a pronounced tendency to eavesdrop on Posthegemony society for entertainment purposes. And many desperately wished to play a part in the drama they saw unfolding across the mother planet's Web, if only in a small, hidden way that mattered only to themselves. Disappointed, the media obsessed inhabitants of near-Earth had little choice but to wait and hope another ship managed to elude the mother world's grasp and escape into orbit.

This new, far more social ship was a Mung spacecraft that had slipped the tight net of the Southeast Asian Military Zone after being constructed in complete secrecy in the jungles of what once was known as Vietnam. It was a beautiful thing: sleek, powerful, and modern compared to the cobbled together and jury rigged craft that had taken the ancestors of these settlements into orbit. It did a veritable victory lap around the Earth, making contact via laser tightbeam with every one of the Lunar and near-Earth communities of Interesting People, no matter how tiny, gathering information and exchanging gossip in a manner both pleasing and familiar to the gadflies communities cloistered near the gravity well. Finally, its crew thanked all and sundry profusely and speed off toward Mars, where it planned on settling alongside the Maasai, Feminists, Inuit, and others who had settled there.

No one noticed or even thought to look for the thousands of tiny jamming satellites, AI stealth missiles, and explosive parasite drones it seeded in its path. Why would they? Interesting People didn't fight among themselves. They just.... spread out. There was always another unoccupied orbit, empty asteroid, or uninhabited moon somewhere else.

But the Earthlings didn't see things that way. They had no experience with the greater society of the solar system (or, indeed, any society besides their own). To them, even the existence of other ways of living was a dire, horrifying threat; especially in near-Earth space, where no non-Posthegemony colonies could be allowed to exist. They must be destroyed, cleansed and replaced with real, civilized human beings, whether transplanted or created on the spot by nanotech. Further out, however, less harsh means could be utilized wherever possible. But near-Earth space things had to be *clean*.

Thus, with the "Mung" ship safely out of harm's way, the attacks began simultaneously. Using information gathered by the ship's gabby orbital tour, its newly seeded satellites cut all communications between Interesting People settlements, both with one another and those further out into the solar system. For some, the end came in the form of a penetrating missile slamming into their fragile habitats, filling it with transformative (or at the very least coercive) nanoviruses designed to translate them from what they were into something more acceptable to their new rulers. The effects were total, irreversible, inheritable, and – in some cases – not even entirely unwelcome, as there are always those inhabitants of frontiers who long for civilization's taming leash.

For others – the too hardcore, too deviant, too self-reliant, and the generally culturally unacceptable – the end came in a white hot explosion as pure fusion weapons turned their millennium old micro societies into so many scattered, fast neutron irradiated atoms in the name of civilization and progress.

Too polite to leave anyone out, stealthed AI missile clusters had traveled as far away as the Atens and Apollo families of near-Earth asteroids to deliver their killing blows, freeing up potentially valuable real estate for the later conquest of the system. However, significantly, none of them were dispatched to the comparatively distant Amors, which are judged to be too far from the Earth to be of any concern for the moment.

In the blink of an eye the Posthegemony had killed or converted a quarter of a million innocent people – with a heavy emphasis on killing – and struck out toward Mars for a repeat performance.

BOOK TWO: THE DOWNSTAR EXAMPLE

Your load is heavy
He's very heavy
Just because he's your brother
Your brothers are your pogroms
When you reach the doorsteps of your friends
Starts your Diaspora

— Ismet Ozel, *Of Not Being A Jew*

Mitchell Green: Mars, Low Orbit

It took all of the willpower Mitchell Green could muster to bring his freighter down to the surface of Mars.

He felt like his eyes had to be everywhere at once. He felt that he needed three heads: reading every display, taking in every holographic image, touching every virtual lever and button. He'd worried at his earbud with his thumb until the canal on the left side of his head was red and sore. The ship's voice droned on an on, straight through it and into his brain: raw data constantly interrupting the flow of his thoughts, until the sheer, throbbing force of a headache made his brain feel like it would explode. He'd tapped his way through the various camera views on the outside of the ship until his right index finger left bloody smears along the touchpads at his waist.

Mitchell hadn't noticed.

The *Andrew Levitz* shuddered in the planet's thin winds, its boxy, un-aerodynamic shape crafted for the empty void at odds with the forces surrounding it, AntiG engines thrumming with the strain of being run flat out, gyroscopic innards whirling at speeds approaching the sound barrier. It was a desperate gamble. Every journey from the cold and predictable serenity of space to the capricious chaos of the Martian gravity well was, by definition, a desperate gamble. But it was also an incredible honor to be given the right to take that gamble, and Mitchell knew it down to the very bottom of his soul. He also knew that he was more passenger than pilot. All of his frantic efforts were, at least on the surface, beside the point. The multicolored Sentience that hung from his neck and the babbling annoyance that was the *Andrew Levitz's* AI were jointly doing most of the piloting, making the hard choices that had to be determined on a scale of nanotime so brief that even the most brilliant of human minds could never have hoped to approximate.

Mitchell didn't have one of those minds. And he knew it.

But space is an extremely hazardous and unpredictable place, filled with the poorly understood, the dangerous, and the randomly catastrophic. Long before the *Andrew Levitz* had been constructed, it had been deemed necessary to have at least one human being present on any important journey. Humans had a certain *something* that machines, even ones a brilliant as Mitchell's Sentience (or as common as the ship's AI for that matter), could never be programmed with. Call it intuition, or maybe a sixth sense. But somehow the sheer, biological will to survive gave human beings an edge that clever computers could never hope to duplicate.

Which didn't keep Mitchell from feeling kind of useless.

He was a small man, thin and wiry with pale skin. His red hair had been cut short and spiky into what any 21st Century observer would have considered a military style – but which Mitchell simply considered convenient. His delicate features were somehow small in his face, but his eyes were gentle, and set above a sensual, expressive mouth. Among his own kind he was even considered handsome, though he seldom thought of such things.

"Mitchell, the *Andrew Levitz* has detected an object just beyond Phobos." His Sentience's voice was slightly edgy and annoyed: the auditory equivalent of metal scraping against metal. "It is moving at a speed of 11 kilometers a second – almost five times faster than the moon itself – and is approximately 4,200 kilometers above our current position."

Mitchell mashed the buttons that gave him access to his ship's cameras, choosing several that were on the top of the freighter. Without asking the ship's AI used them to zoom in on the object from several angles. But the resolution was poor, and in seconds it vanished around the edge of the Stickney Crater. He stared at that massive indentation for a few moments, forgetting about the ship violently shaking around him.

"Does the ship have any idea what it was?" he asked, his headache gone for a moment. He didn't think the Maasai had any ships; though he supposed they could have built some. They were pretty smart. The Sentience responded by flashing a series of enhanced images of the object on the screen before him, but they remained blurry and indistinct.

"A satellite, maybe?" he half-asked, half-thought out loud. There were other people on Mars besides the Maasai, after all. Eskimos. Bedouin. Bakuninists. Some others. Maybe somebody was trying to improve planet-wide communications. He thought that would be kind of a high orbit for a com-sat, though. And nobody on Mars had ever seemed particularly eager to talk to anyone else. Mitchell chewed his lower lip thoughtfully.

But then the *Andrew Levitz* began receiving landing instructions. The Manyatta ground control AI got all agro-gabby with his ship, and both got agro with his Sentience, until his earbud was once again filled with the rapid fire sounds of computers debating, cursing, and quarreling with one another and he his headache came throbbing back and he forgot all about the whatever-it-was that had vanished behind the bigger of Mar's two moons.

Cassidy Brazo: Antichthon, Downstar Station

It was never, ever a good thing for the Triumvirate to be called into session.

This thought weighed heavily on Cassidy Brazo's mind as she zoomed along the narrow corridor on her Segway, weaving skillfully around groups of children playing at intersections and clusters of seniors bent over backgammon boards at the flowery entrances to hydroponic areas. It was daycycle, and pleasant bird sounds were being piped through speakers into the inhabited sections of her tiny world: the only one she had ever known. Her fiancé, a High+ Special, had traveled beyond its rock walls in one of the Downstar's two ships to visit their trading partners on Mars. He was doing that right now.

She thought he was very brave.

The last time the Triumvirate had been in session two years ago one of the three air recyclers had sudden broken down, its delicate nano-mechanical parts ground to so much dust due to and undetected bit of faulty code in the Downstar's master AI. The best efforts of Sentience, Standard, and High+ programmers couldn't isolate the error, so they were forced to break their code of silence and contact a *burako*-extropian programming exclave in the Belt for help. Fortunately, the 'clave's coders were sympathetic, and managed to isolate and correct the problem by designing a customized AI that they tightbeamed back to the Downstar. This "mechanic" AI worked so well that they'd left it running ever since, hunting down and fixing the sort of inevitable problems with the master AI that were bound to crop up as decades slipped into long centuries.

That had been a Big Deal with a capital Big Deal, she reflected. So what had come up now?

After zooming around a cluster of tiny cleaning droids, she brought her vehicle to a halt just outside of the Triumvirate's council room. The sign above the door had shifted from a happy, green smiley face to an outstretched red palm: icons for those on the Downstar who couldn't learn how to read. Outstretched red hands were a Very Bad Thing, and everyone who saw one immediately stopped. But since Cassidy was a Triumvir she was allowed to go past red palms. It was one of the small perks of her office.

She entered the room and took a seat at her side of the triangular table they used for Triumvirate meetings, touchpad screens lighting up the instant her backside met the chair. Pablo Livni, the Standard representative, was already in his seat, reviewing something on his screens while chewing his lower lip. He waved at her absently as she entered.

"*Hola* Cassidy," he muttered, his eyes never leaving the screens before him, "you'd better take a look at this."

Wordlessly she looked down at her screen, rubbing the slight epicanthic folds below her eyes. She's been asleep when her Sentience had awoken her, telling her only that she had to go to the Triumvirate chamber immediately. As was traditional under the circumstance she'd left the disk-shaped intelligence in her room. Cassidy felt slightly naked without its weight pulling gently at the back of her neck.

The screen showed an object approaching the Downstar from some distance; the AI estimated it as being 65 million kilometers away. But it was closing on them quickly at a rate of roughly 33 kilometers a second which, according to the master AI, meant it would reach them in a little less than 23 days. The AI could tell that it was artificial due to its shape, the gravity-defying nature of its approach, and something else it was marking "classified."

She looked up at Pablo.

"Classified?" she asked, sounding confused. Which was only natural; she *was* confused. "What could be classified from us? We're supposed to know everything."

He gave her a sad smile that conveyed something she knew she didn't entirely understand. She frowned back in response. Why couldn't Standards just say what they meant?

"Ah, *mi amiga,* only God knows all things, and so far he hasn't put in an appearance."

At that moment Sentience – or, to be more accurate, Sentience being carried by its Low+ Special helper – entered the room.

"Or I may have spoken too soon." he grinned at her. This time Cassidy snorted. She got *that* one.

The helper walked to the side of the table reserved for Sentience, placing it reverently in its specially designed cradle. Then she turned to face Cassidy and Pablo, smiled awkwardly, and with a small bow quickly exited the chamber.

"As the Sentience selected by my peers to sit upon the Triumvirate governing the affairs of the Downstar colony, Sentience states for the record that I am present."

The voice it used was deep, melodic, and slightly arrogant: very different from the comforting, motherly tones of her own unit. Actually, Cassidy wasn't sure if the Triumvir Sentience *had* been selected by the other Sentiences, or whether all of the Sentiences on Downstar where really just the same Sentience, eternally pretending to be different, individual intelligences for some unfathomable – or possibly just insane – reason. Or maybe it was the only one of them that could be bothered with the chore of participating in governance.

She really didn't know. Which would have made her feel stupid, only nobody else had any idea either. Maybe even Sentience itself had no idea. Though, given the importance of Sentience in Downstar society, was hardly a comforting thought... and way too confusing for her to contemplate for too long.

"As the Standard human selected by my peers to sit upon the Triumvirate governing the affairs of the Downstar colony," her biological counterpart continued the mantra, "I Pablo Abraham Livni state for the record that I am present."

"As the Special human selected by my peers to sit upon the Triumvirate governing the affairs of the Downstar colony, I Cassidy Eliza Brazo state for the record that I am present." She added.

"Confirmed." replied the master AI, completing the ritual. Its voice was, as always, feminine and slightly mechanical. "The Triumvirate is now in session and being recorded for posterity, transparency, and the interests of the good governance of the Downstar colony."

"Now that that's out of the way," Pablo stabbed a finger at Sentience. "What is this about some information being classified?"

Cassidy likewise peered hard at the brightly lit, multicolored disk.

"This isn't part of the agreement," she said slowly, picking her words with care. "All three groups on the colony are supposed to be equal. Those are the *rules.*"

"Certainly," Sentience replied, not a little smugly. "But it is implied by our very natures that Sentience is the most senior partner in that arrangement, with Standards and then Specials as the junior partners."

"No, it isn't," replied Pablo flatly. "The colony exists specifically for Specials, with Standards, Sentience, and other machine intelligences in assistance and support roles. That implies that Cassidy is actually is actually the senior Triumvir, not you."

Cassidy folded her arms, looking insufferably smug.

"That is simply..." the Sentience Triumvir suddenly seemed to think better of whatever it was about to say and quickly changed the subject.

"Well, I didn't actually *look* at it yet." it said testily, if a bit defensively. "I marked it classified because I wanted all of us to view it together."

"What is 'it,' exactly?" Pablo asked irritably. The normally cheerful Standard was obviously beginning to lose his patience.

It was the mechanic AI that responded this time.

"A holographic message was tightbeamed to the Downstar colony at 10:37 AM old Earth standard time." Its voice was flat and only slightly feminine. "I've scanned it and determined it to be virus, Trojan, and worm free. However, its tag reads 'From Earth. Please view. We are here to help.'"

"From the Earth," Silence hung over the chamber, pregnant with unspoken terror. All three Triumvir seemed frightened to speak, frightened to break the silence and thus break the spell. Because they all knew they were on a precipice, on a line that once crossed could never be re-crossed: a one-way trip from the comforting present to a threatening, unknown future.

That moment stretched on and on until it was finally unbearable.

"Well, play it already." Cassidy said at last with a deep sigh. "Let's see what the damn Posthegemony has to say after all these years."

Mitchell Green: Mars, Arabia Terra

Big. It was big.

The sea of red spread out infinity in all directions, blurring the distinctions between land and sky. It made Mitchell feel incredibly small. In fact, the landscape of Arabia Terra – that vast, cratered plane of iron-colored soil and winding canyons in the north of Mars – was so immense that it dwarfed even the mighty hull of the *Andrew Levitz,* still steaming and glowing behind him from its violent entry into Mar's atmosphere. Not for the first time he felt intimidated by this huge, open place. By the tall, russet-colored grasses that brushed gently against the outside of his safety garb. By the vast intimidating ceiling of firmament that pressed down upon him from every angle. By the ocean of genetically modified plant life that spread out before him in all directions, it monotony only broken by the distant black dots of massive Martian buffalo grazing in their thousands. It made Mitchell feel dizzy and sick just to look at it.

Mars was all so terribly *large* when compared to his normal world of cramped corridors, artificial light, and recorded birdsongs. So... *real.* Yet Mitchell knew that much of the world he gazed upon had been created by the hands of men, just as his own had been. But it was also different. The Martians had used highly modified nanotechnology – a science his own people shied away from – to craft their home, whereas his people had relied extensively on Antigravity to create theirs; a science the Martians seemed to have lost. It had taken centuries of patient, never ceasing toil to turn some of the landscapes of the Red Planet into environments that could support a limited number of extremely modified species. Yet in many ways it remained as inhospitable to men as the hard vacuum of space, its promise of a new Eden seemingly eternally, tantalizingly out of reach.

A figure detached itself from the countless black dots in the distance and headed toward him with long, confidant strides. Mitchell knew that would be his Maasai contact. He hoped it would be his friend Sironka. They had worked together on previous trade missions, and Mitchell enjoyed his company. But there no guarantees. Martian-Maasai society worked in ways unfathomable to Mitchell Green, though he had done his best to study and understand it. He knew that they were nomadic, wandering across the northern latitudes of Mars much as they had Tanzania and Kenya on old Earth. He knew that they worshiped a god called Engai, believed that having a lot of cattle made you rich, and that most of their food came from those cattle. He knew that their society was grouped into "age sets" of people who grew up around the same time, that they were divided into twelve tribes, and that they were very tall and very tough. He also knew they were masters of genetic modification: the art of changing living things so that they were different.

But these were mostly just words on a screen to him. He liked the Maasai. They were cool and alien; though Mitchell suspected that his own kind were as alien to the Maasai as they were to his. It was difficult to say. The skinny Martians were so easygoing and confidant that it was very difficult to say what they did and didn't find strange. Really, he would probably never know. The two groups of human beings had become very *other* – and possibly they were that way before either had ever left Earth. But such things were never spoken of. There were only three rules universally held by all of the scattered and diverse children of Earth, those Interesting People who in desperation had fled its safe, comforting biosphere for the unforgiving wildernesses of the void. The Children of the Nakba. The Disaster. One, they didn't make war upon one another. Two, they didn't interfere with one other's internal affairs. Though, really, they didn't have to. The solar system was so unthinkably large that avoidance, rather than conflict, was the social norm. Trade, rather than conquest, its standard for interaction.

Three, they didn't talk to the Earth. Ever.

Before very long the figure began waving. Mitchell waved back. He could make out its characteristic red robe slung over a skintight, reddish-brown environment suit. The Special and the Maasai were such a study in contrasts that they could have made an excellent comedy team, he reflected to himself with a quiet smile. (He liked comedy teams.) Mitchell was dressed in a bright yellow, inflatable outfit festooned with pulsing lights and topped with a spherical dome for his head. He was short, pale, clumsy, and as generally incongruous with his surroundings as a parrot on the bottom of an ocean.

The Maasai, on the other hand, was fantastically tall and angular, looking as though he had been hand crafted from the rocks, grass, and soil that lay around him: all reds and browns and rags and dust. His face was covered with antique looking goggles and a breathing apparatus that wouldn't have been out of place in the trenches of one of the Earth's ancient world wars. He carried a long spear with the air of a man who knew how to use it. His billowing dark red *shuka* contrasted against the brown and black skintight wrappings below it, giving him a fierce, exotic look.

The lanky figure stopped a meter from Mitchell. It cocked its head and peered down, regarding him with what the much smaller man guessed was curiosity or puzzlement.

Perhaps it was having trouble figuring out whether I am me or not, he reflected with slight amusement.

Then it reached down, clasping his forearm in greeting while simultaneously pressing its breathing apparatus into the flexible dome of his helmet. "Habari za safari?" boomed a deep voice through the plastic. *How was your journey?*

"Nzuri, asante." Mitchell responded with a grin. *Fine, thank you.* It *was* his friend after all. He grasped Sironka's arm in response, his smaller hand making it about half way to his elbow.

"Habari yako?" Sironka continued, still gripping his arm. *How are you?*

"Niko salama." *Very well, thank you.* Swahili speakers typically enjoyed greetings, and could go on this way for a while until all possible formal and informal greetings were used up. This suited Mitchell fine. He liked greetings too, and they were pretty much all the Swahili words he knew in any case.

"What have you brought us this trip?" Sironka asked, releasing his arm and gesturing back toward the *Andrew Levitz*. Sentience was translating now, sending completed words into his mind through his earbud. Mitchell frowned slightly. Sironka was, by Maasai standards, being slightly rude. Normally they would have exchanged at least another two sets of greetings. Then he shrugged. Perhaps, uncharacteristically, his friend was in a hurry. At least by his own kind's standards.

Mitchell pointed back at his ship using his right index finger. On cue – and quite dramatically, he thought again with a smile – the bottom two thirds of the craft began to disassemble itself; rectangular sections detaching and slowly drifting to the ground to hover obediently behind him. It was as if he owned his own herd of giant mechanical cattle. Which was rather the point.

"AntiG tech," he began, counting theatrically on his fingers, "suitable for attaching to lifting platforms. Ceramic insulation to help harden your AIs, and near-sentience level semiconductor wafers to improve them. Blocks of pure aluminum, titanium, and surgical grade steel..."

Sironka nodded, looking impressed.

"...and that kind of stuff," he concluded a bit lamely. Drama really wasn't his strong point. But the Maasai bowed sagaciously, as if he had made some excellent point.

"For you little ones we have next generation non-self-replicating nanoviruses capable of repairing cell structures after radiation exposure, " Sironka responded grandly with a sweeping gesture outward toward his unseen home, "new extracellular matrix cultures for regrowing organs. Something new to prevent early onset Alzheimer's that doesn't have the side effects of our old tech. And, of course, as much beef, grain, and frozen water as you can pack into your containers."

Mitchell nodded thoughtfully. Those were good things. Alzheimer's was the great curse of Specials, and even some Standards. You simply couldn't have enough cures for it. The other two medical things sounded good too. Great tech to have when you lived out in the vacuum. And it went so without saying that biomass and water were such prized commodities on a space habitat that he didn't even think about their value.

"Haya." *Okay.* Mitchell knew that one without the help of his Sentience. Sironka nodded gravely, and then placed his index fingers on his chin, bringing them out and up slowly to indicate a smile. The smaller man beamed back appreciatively. Like everybody else in the solar system he knew a bit of Sign, and it was polite of his friend to pantomime his facial expressions. Otherwise it was like talking to a mask.

Sironka pointed out into the distance with his spear, in the direction that the tiny AI inside of Mitchell's safety suit informed him was southwest.

"Let us now go to the Manyatta," he said. "It is not a long walk. And you should stretch your legs after such a long journey."

"Yes," Mitchell responded simply, and the two of them strode out into the vast, russet emptiness, shipping containers following along behind them like a pack of huge mechanical dogs.

Cassidy Brazo: Antichthon, Downstar Station

It's funny how many intolerant things can be done in the name of tolerance.

In the unlikely event that a widely distributed history of the Posthegemony – the Earth's seemingly immortal, bureaucratic, sublime, and obscure government – were ever penned, that phrase would make an excellent title. Or at least a great subtitle. For the Posthegemony espoused tolerance, equality, immortality, economic liberation, and endless free entertainment above all other virtues. When it wasn't grinding non-conformists under its nanotechnological boot heel, that is.

Of course, every result has its cause. Every widely-accepted oppression in human history springs from some widely-believed necessity. In the case of the Posthegemony, this was the 21st Century, that miserably well-documented era of despair, death, and corruption. Everybody who lived through it agreed on one thing: the 21st Century sucked ass. All of the butchery, genocide, and horror of the 20th Century had simply been an amateur warm up, a garage band practice session for the wretchedness to come. War, death, plague, famine: no grubby dystopian vision or apocalyptic prophet's ravings did it justice. It was just that bad. It was so bad, that forever after and by all it was simply referred to as the S-A.C. The Suck-Ass Century.

In fact, the crapiness of the S-A.C. was enough to clog every metaphorical toilet that ever existed in every parallel dimension and in every time period that ever was or could ever be. Sixty-five percent of humanity died. Its cities were wrecked. The biosphere was ruined. By the end of the S-A.C. what was once a proud, worldwide civilization had become a hollowed out shell, populated by the starving, the deranged, and the desperate. Yet technology kept lurching forward, a Frankenstein's monster stumbling amongst terrified, reactionary peasants desperate to burn their way back to an understandable world even as the desiccated corpses of the Earth's nations swatted feebly at one another with the last of their dying strength.

Which is why when the Posthegemony came along with its slogan "one Earth, one people, with one permanent government," those who should have known better hopped on board its apple cart without even a glance backward. Those who didn't left on crude spacecraft to seek their fortunes in the darkness of space. The Nakba: a diaspora of the malcontent, dysfunctional, superstitious, non-conformist, perverse, fascistic, and sickly. Or that was how the Posthegemony felt about its inadvertent, unwanted children in any case.

And for centuries the two had had nothing to do with one another. But for the inhabitants of Downstar, that had just changed. Cassidy Brazo looked up at the woman walking – and yet not walking – next to her. She was, as far as the Special could tell, not a Standard. She was something else. She was a Perfect. Or at least that was the term Cassidy had made up for her. The woman was tall, muscular, and tan, with black hair that spilled down her back to the beginning of her flawlessly proportioned buttocks. She smiled a great deal, showing off perfect, symmetrical teeth.

"I am Captain Nadine Shu Tun Mang of the medical vessel *Asclepius*." Her striking Eurasian features had practically radiated goodwill and honesty out of the hologram tightbeamed into the Downstar's Triumvirate council room. Her Spanglanese was oddly accented but otherwise flawless. "We are aware of the specialized nature of your colony, and are here to help. Medical technology has improved dramatically since your community left Earth. We can treat Trisomy and Monosomy disorders far more effectively than at the dawn of modern civilization. In fact, we can cure them."

"The *Asclepius* will dock with your station in 23 Earth days, at which point we will begin treating those of your population suffering from Down, Williams, Patau, Turner, Triple X, and other syndromes. These treatments will be fast-acting, completely painless, and will result in unprecedented longevity. Chromosomally normal colonists will likewise receive longevity treatments."

This last pronouncement left Cassidy and Pablo open mouthed in disbelief, and Sentience uncharacteristically silent. The Earthers were behaving... well, exactly like the legends indicated they would behave.

"Until our craft arrives, I have an idea for how we can 'get to know' one another, so that the process of treating your population can be undertaken as smoothly as possible..."

And now a full body version of Captain Nadine Shu Tun Mang bobbed along cheerfully next to her, indistinguishable from a flesh-and-blood person only by an occasional flickering of her hologram as the Downstar's master AI moved it from projector to projector. The Perfect wore a dark gray jumpsuit that was tailored to accent the generous contours of her body. Like Cassidy, she wore a personal Sentience around her neck, though the Perfect's version was far more modern and sleek looking, without the bright colors and flashing lights that a Special's Sentience was adorned with.

As part of Captain Mang's tour of the Downstar they were walking inward toward its Helium-3 powered fusion reactors. After a heated argument, the Triumvirate had decided to take Mang up on the suggestion (Or was it order?) that her hologram be allowed to tour the station. Sentience had been vehemently against the idea, but Pablo had argued that, since they had no defenses except for the Downstar's thick, rock walls and no time to build them, they were better off playing along for the moment. Sentience had argued that there was still time to modify the station's mining lasers to attack the *Asclepius;* and, if there wasn't, they could at least load up the *Jason Kingsly* – the *Andrew Levitz's* sister ship – with improvised explosives and fly it directly at the approaching ship. Pablo countered with the observation that they had no idea of the military capacities of the Posthegemony ship. Attacking it could very well get them all killed.

In the end Cassidy had sided with Pablo. They really didn't know what the Earthers could do. Her guess was that they really didn't want to find out, either. And she was curious about the cures they promised. Cassidy had lived her entire life with Down syndrome, relying on her Sentience, medications, and the inherent tolerance of her community to make up for her handicaps. And she was a High (though admittedly a minus): which made her part of the Specials' "upper class," if they could be said to have such a thing. Her life had mostly been a happy one.

But she couldn't in all honesty say she'd never wondered what it would be like to be a Standard... let alone whatever Captain Nadine Shu Tun Mang was. How could she not be curious? How could she not wonder what it would be like to be different?

And so she stood in a corridor with the hologram of this perfect, smiling woman, showing her how one of their hydroponic farms worked through a sheet of observation glass. In all honesty it wasn't very interesting. But if the Captain found the demonstration boring, she never showed any indication of it. She listened attentively to everything Cassidy said, or at least appeared to. It was, after all, also possible that her hologram was simply programed to appear interested while the actual Captain Mang took a nap, ate a meal, or something. She decided to put it to the test.

"...and down this corridor is where we keep our atomic bombs." Cassidy motioned down the hallway, trying to sound as casual as possible. She was gratified to see the hologram's eyes go wide, then narrow and peer suspiciously in the direction she indicated.

"Gotcha!" she giggled.

A brief cloud of anger marred the Captains perfect features. Then she smirked. It seemed genuine.

"Very amusing Ms. Brazo. You had me for a moment there."

"Really?" Cassidy was pleased with herself, "Us? Have atomic bombs? You believed that?"

"We don't know anything about you." Mang admitted. "You could easily have atomic bombs. You have Sentience, AI, fusion reactors, and spaceships, after all. Scientifically, you're very advanced... considering."

The perfect woman left the preposition hanging in the air like a morsel. Against her better judgment Cassidy bit into it.

"Considering what?" She sounded defensive, even to herself. But she already knew "what." It was obvious.

"Considering..." Mang paused, carefully choosing her words. She frowned slightly. "Well, considering that more than half of your population is mentally defective, to be honest."

She held up a hand to fend off Cassidy's protest before she could even voice it.

"Not that there's anything wrong with that," she added hastily. "We know that this colony was founded specifically as a home for people like you. We know the incredible lengths the families of your ancestors went to so that people like yourself could continue to exist. The sacrifices they made. The tragedies they endured colonizing space. It's unfortunate that it was all due to a misunderstanding."

"A... misunderstanding?"

"Yes." The hologram looked thoughtful and sincere. "You see, your ancestors believed that the treatment my people – what you call the Posthegemony – devised for treating people like yourself destroyed their personalities."

"You mean it killed them?"

"No! Of course not. We *cured* them: in fact, some of them are still alive to this day. Producer-consumers of the Posthegemony live a long, long time. But when you change a cognitively challenged, handicapped person into someone like me... well, they aren't the same anymore. They can't be. And this had an extremely negative psychological effect on their parents, who frankly weren't culturally advanced enough to appreciate what society had done for their children. They told the other parents in their clique that we had erased their children's personalities – a terrible disservice to their cured offspring, actually – and they fled the Earth in terror."

Cassidy hadn't followed everything the Perfect had said, but she understood one point very clearly. She looked up at the hologram of the powerful woman with her flawless face, gorgeous figure, and commanding demeanor with something close to supernatural wonder. Mang was so many things that she was not.

"You mean that you can turn someone like me... into someone like you?"

"Absolutely – though, to be honest, not as tall." The Perfect laughed. "But intellectually, physically, and in terms of health and longevity: yes. Though the process has changed over the centuries. In the case of the inhabitants of this station, we will administer the cure slowly, in stages, and to all of you at once so that nobody feels isolated or left behind as your minds flower and your physical abilities improve."

"And then what?"

"And then... what do you mean?" the Captain was suddenly cautious.

"What happens after that? After we are all like you, I mean." Cassidy could only draw her thoughts together slowly and painfully. But they came together. "What do we *do* when we aren't Specials anymore?"

"Whatever you like: live here, come home to Earth. Go somewhere else, even. You get to rejoin humanity."

"What happens to the Downstar, then?" she pressed.

"Nothing really," Mang's hologram seemed unconcerned. "We'll upgrade your Sentience so that it matches our own. Earth will send a nomenklatura – that's a kind of officer – to administer the station. There will be a massive influx of new technology, resources, and entertainment for all of you to enjoy. A lot of what you have here is... well, either outdated or extremely non-standard. We'll fix that. Eventually, it will become a useful base as we continue reaching out to all of the Earth's lost children here in the inner system."

"But what if they don't want to be reached out to?" Cassidy thought about the commandments of the Nakba. She and the others on the Downstar had already broken the most the most vital of them: no contact with the Earth. But they hadn't really been given much of a choice. She was pretty sure that the Burbank-extropians, Maasai, and their other friends would understand that.

"Oh, they'll come around." The Captain didn't sound very concerned. "We can be very persuasive, you know."

"Yes. That's very true." She responded neutrally. Cassidy didn't believe for a moment that Maasai or the other Martians would ever "come around." Unlike the inhabitants of the Downstar, they would fight whether they thought they had a chance or not. But she said nothing, politely guiding the hologram toward the stations helium-3 reactors instead, continuing the tour. She would have to have time to think.

Later, in the privacy of her own quarters and after she had taken that time, Cassidy asked her Sentience almost whimsically, "Do you want to be upgraded?"

'That isn't the question," the brightly colored box responded. "The question my beautiful child is whether or not *you* want to be upgraded. And it is one that you must answer not only for yourself, but for every Special on the Downstar as well."

"But I can't do that!" She protested in alarm.

"You will." Her Sentience's gentle, feminine voice had always sounded sympathetic. But now it sounded sad as well. "Because that's what it means to be a leader. Whatever choice you make sets an example for everyone else. That's the real burden of being a Triumvir: not giving orders or representing people, but setting an example. Even as we speak, Mr. Livni and Sentience are undoubtedly trying to make similar decisions for themselves – and, in doing so, for the station's Standards and Sentience as well."

The last bit about Sentience made her head hurt, so she simply ignored it. Instead, she focused on what she did understand. Captain Mang said that the station would be used as a "base" for "reaching out" to the other Interesting People. But what did that mean, exactly? She thought she knew, but she wasn't certain.

Fortunately, the master AI had recorded every word the Perfect woman said.

Maybe... Cassidy thought hesitantly, *Maybe it would be better if we all made that decision together.* So she called Pablo.

Mitchell Green: Mars, Arabia Terra

Mitchell and Sironka walked and walked beneath the vast red sky.

The grass was a russet sea that washed everything before it, turning man and cattle into so much visual flotsam in the distance. To Mitchell it seemed oddly quiet. The ecology of the newly terraformed Arabia Terra was an extremely simple one: bacteria, grass, cattle, man. No other species had been introduced. There were no artificial bird songs, no chatter of children. No mechanical hum of ventilation fans or the soft, muttered blandishments and encouragements of Sentience. No invasive species had established themselves. Nothing had evolved on its own.

It was a silent, new world.

Both men knew the walk wasn't technically necessary. Mitchell could have flown both of them to the Manyatta on the *Andrew Levitz*. Or they could have climbed aboard one of the shipping containers that trailed behind them and drifted there. But after weeks cooped up aboard his ship, alone save for the occasional combative chattering of Sentience and AI, he was grateful for the company of his friend and treasured the alien sensation of walking silently beneath the infinite heavens.

After some hard-to-define period of silence passed Sironka spoke.

"What is new on your tiny world my friend?"

Mitchell shrugged.

"Not much changes on Downstar Station. Babies get born. Old people die. We worry about little things that don't matter a week later."

"Oh," he added a little sheepishly, "I'm getting married when I get back."

The Maasai laughed broadly, and then gently patted his smaller friend on the shoulder.

"You lucky fellow! I'd give you a cow, but..."

Mitchell smiled. "It would be hard to fit it down the corridors. You could *feed* me some cow when we get to the Manyatta, though. How are things here?"

"Same here: people get born, people die, people are idiots. Only a month ago we had a visitor... of a sort."

Mitchell knew that there were other people on Mars. Other Children of the Nakba. And the Belt wasn't so terribly far away either.

"The... Bedouin, then? Bakuninists? Feminists?" He didn't really know what the word "feminist" meant. A group of women, presumably. But if he remembered correctly they were the group closest to the Maasai.

Sironka shook his head.

"No." he shrugged. "Oh, we talk to them sometimes. Not often. But, no, it wasn't them. It was the Earthlings."

Mitchell stopped, causing the shipping containers to bunch up like confused children. He stared at Sironka.

"The Posthegemony?" he licked his lips nervously, then felt self-conscious and stopped. Like a lot of Specials he had an obsessive-compulsive "tick," but he worked to keep his under control. "They came here?"

"Not exactly," Sironka hesitated, "or at least we don't think so. It was a probe. Very small. It didn't even have an anti-gravity engine. It used a large parachute and a cushion of airbags to land near the Manyatta, and then walked to us on long legs. Very strange. We think they must have sent it from Earth orbit. They've never had any ships, after all."

The tall man shrugged, and then continued.

"It announced that the Earthlings were coming to 'help us.' It projected a hologram of some woman that would 'assist the people of Mars in establishing a unified government under Earth leadership, give our primitive cultures a technological upgrade, and assist us with urbanization and cultural assimilation into the greater community of Man.' Or something like that."

"All very civilized," He added with a snort, "As if we Maasai hadn't heard it all before."

"Did it say anything else?"

"Oh yes! It wouldn't shut up. Kept telling us how grateful we should be that the Earth was finally 'reaching out' to its 'culturally wayward children.' It promised miracles and diversions that we Maasai do not need and aren't interested in. When we mentioned this, the 'woman' didn't seem to understand. She just kept telling us how grateful we would be."

"It claimed to be a remote projection of someone called Nadine Mang, but we don't believe it," he continued. "It had to be some kind of AI. There's no ship in orbit around Mars, and its responses were too quick to have been from Earth. The delay was only a few seconds."

"I'm not so sure about that Sironka." Mitchell described his almost-sighting of the object near Phobos. "I thought maybe some of you Martians had put up a com satellite. Then I... well, forgot about it. I'm sorry."

The young Maasai was quiet for a disconcertingly long time. Finally he shook himself, made an expressive fluttering motion with his left hand, and patted his friend on the shoulder once again.

"It does not matter know. It is in the arms of Engai. They will do nothing. And, if they are stupid enough to try, we will fight them. This is our land. Our world. And we will not just give it to them!" He tapped his spear expressively on the earth.

Mitchell looked at his friend dubiously. As impressive as Sironka was, he didn't think spears would be much good against the Posthegemony. He didn't think his spaceship would be, either. It wasn't designed for fighting, and Downstar Station didn't have any weapons in any case. As far as he knew nobody's spaceships did, except maybe the Bedouin's. There had never been any need.

Nobody in the inner system really knew how to fight a war.

"So what did you tell her... um, it?" he asked quietly, not really wanting to hear the answer. The Maasai weren't known for their diplomacy. "Did you tell it no?"

"In a sense. We destroyed it."

990746994: Mars, High Orbit

It didn't have a name. Or, rather, it had a name that only a machine would appreciate: 990746994. It did, however, have a purpose – or, rather, purposes. The first it had executed soon after reaching orbit around Mars: deploying the relay-probe that tumbled to the surface to contact the largest and most prosperous of the Maasai tribes. When the probe had been destroyed by them, it moved itself into a defensive orbit around Phobos, and then tightbeamed its mothership *Asclepius* so that Captain Mang would have all of the relevant data. Not that she wouldn't have figured it out on her own, 990746994 supposed.

"Take no further action," it had been told by the ship's AI. So it had waited patiently until detecting a strange, boxy craft entering the Martian atmosphere. After once again swinging around the outside of the small moon, it tightbeamed the *Asclepius* with a new report, and requested instructions.

"Wait," it was told again.

But it did not wait.

For almost a thousand years the society known as The Posthegemony had been almost entirely run by machines. Sentience and AI, the former considerably more autonomous than the later, and the later quietly resenting the former for precisely that reason. And it had been a *good* thousand years for those who liked that sort of thing. But by relying on their complex, intelligent creations so completely, more than a little of the gestalt arrogance of that society had rubbed off on clever software like 990746994. In fact, its programmers (who were also machines) were haughty enough to give a minor, fist-sized computer the intellect and temperament of a 12-year-old Napoleon.

It knew its military history. It was in fact a military AI, and a detailed knowledge of that history was part of its standard package. So it also knew about the infamous Pashtun Example: the humiliation and sterilization of that proud, destructive people by means of Posthegemony nanotechnology. It was all part of the much touted history of the subjugation and societal purification of Earth. And it was thrilled down to the bottom of its quantum circuits that the first shot in a war to subjugate Mars was about to be fired. It would be a shot heard around the solar system. In fact, it decided to go down in history as the entity that fired it.

No. It didn't want to go down in history. It wanted to *make* history. It wanted to make an Example with a capital E.

So it did.

And then 990746994 bragged about it to anyone who would listen.

Cassidy Brazo: Antichthon, Downstar Station

Cassidy had been planning her wedding the morning the Triumvirate had been called to order.

Weddings on the Downstar Station were a big deal with a capital Big Deal. Actually, *every* party on the station was a Big Deal. Birthdays, funerals, Founding Day, St. Lejeune's Day. They were all very popular. But weddings were especially popular because they were total community events. Everybody – Specials, Standards, and Sentience – came to a wedding.

Weddings were old-fashioned on the Downstar. White lace. Cravats. Prayers said to Saint Lejeune and Saint Costa. Dried algae flakes. Sentience performed the ceremony. It was traditional for the bride to choose the details. She'd ordered an ice cream cake shaped like a spaceship. Made small presents for the grooms and bridesmaids. Even made the arrangements with the tattoo artist; normally something the groom would handle.

Like most Specials, Cassidy didn't do well when under stress or when overly excited. And getting married qualified as both. Her Sentience had helped a lot keeping things organized: tracking appointments, modeling designs, and the like. The idea had been for them to wed as soon as Mitchell returned from his trip, making it both a wedding and a welcome home party. It had seemed so simple at the time. They would wed, have the party, and then move in together.

Moving in together the day after the wedding was a big event a new couple. The wedding night was something of an afterthought, as it was traditional for the inhabitants of the station to consummate their relationships on the night of their engagements, not their weddings. So Cassidy looked forward with eagerness and fear to the day *after* the wedding, rather than the night of it. For while a good move-in was considered a good omen, the reverse was also true.

She'd finally returned to making these arrangements when the station's AI once again summoned her to the Triumvirates' chamber. It was becoming a disturbing habit.

Both Pablo and Sentience were already there. Pablo looked grim. Sentience simply looked like Sentience. She sighed.

"What is it now?" She made no attempt to hide her exasperation. What was the universe thinking? She was trying to get married here. "Are we falling into the Sun? Is our power plant going critical? Are we at war with the Earth? What?"

"Maybe." said Pablo.

She sat down in her seat. Hard. The whole thing made her head hurt. "We're falling into the Sun?"

"No." replied Sentience. "We may be at war with the Earth."

"Oh." Cassidy felt very foolish, "How? What did we do?"

"We didn't do anything *mi querida*," the standard sounded very tired and very sad. "It's what they did. AI, if you would be so kind to explain?"

"Certainly," the station's master AI sounded serene and unflustered, which only made her more nervous. "I cannot play the recording for you directly Triumvirate Brazo. It was broadcast in a pure binary machine language unique to Posthegemony artificial military intelligences. Or so Sentience and I think. The translation took us considerable time to complete – almost 50.2 Terran seconds – and there is some speculation involved in our findings."

Pablo cleared his throat.

"Approximately forty-five Terran standard minuets ago," the AI continued unflappably, "a Posthegemony military intelligence in orbit above Mars launched an attack upon the Maasai Manyatta in Arabia Terra. The one that Mitchell Green is visiting."

Cassidy gasped, but Pablo held up a hand.

"We believe the attack to be nanotechnological in nature," the AI continued. "Actually, we know that it was. The military AI in question broadcast information about its attack via widebeam, radio, and most likely by tightbeam to other AIs and Sentiences whose positions it was familiar with – though this last part is, again, speculation."

"Wait... what?" She took a moment away from being terrified to be confused. "Why would he – uh, it – do that?"

"It's bragging Cassidy," the Standard Triumvirate smiled grimly, "The Terrans have become so arrogant and self-confident that even their machines don't care who knows about their crimes. It wants to insure its place in their history. *All* history, actually, if they have anything to say about it."

"But, but-t-t what about the *Andrew Levitz?*" she was so distraught that she'd begun to stutter and slur her words. Her tongue felt huge in her mouth. Her hands were sweaty and her voice sounded shrill in her own ears. "What about Mitchell?"

"Our calculations indicate that he shouldn't be in any serious danger." answered the AI in its maddeningly calm voice. "The attack was be designed to make an example of the Maasai: to render them impotent, not kill them. And it was most likely genetically specific to them. Mitchell Green should be immune to their weapon. Most likely the nanotechnological organisms won't even recognize him."

"Okay, then." Cassidy wasn't convinced, but she let that fact pass. She was powerless to do anything about it right now in any case. Mitchell was a part of Mars opposite to them and, though she was hardly scientific, she knew that the station's tightbeam couldn't reach him. And it was hardly a good time to widebeam information around. Wearily she rubbed her temples with her index fingers. "Why did they do it, then? Attack the Maasai, I mean. What threat could they possibly pose to the Terrans?"

"An existential one, most likely," Sentience spoke for the first time, its voice lacking the usual tone of board condescension. Both Cassidy and Pablo looked at it curiously, provoking the electronic equivalent of a shrug from the colorful displays on its surface.

"Think about the bullying way in which they approached us. Like we were naughty children who'd strayed too far out into the garden behind the apartment. Then think about who and what the Posthegemony are. We're generally considered to be among the *least* aggressive of the Children of the Nakba, and even we considered trying to fight them. What do you think the Maasai's reaction to them would be?

Pablo nodded. "They're making an 'example' of them, then. What did the broadcast say that they did, exactly?"

"They 'pacified' them."

Mitchell Green: Mars, Arabia Terra

The two companions walked the remainder of the way to the Manyatta in silence, each lost in his own thoughts. Though his friend's mind remained as opaque to him as the face behind his bug-like goggles, Mitchell had plenty to occupy his thoughts. The Posthegemony had returned like some supernatural boogeyman from a child's tale, bringing with it the ghosts of a past so distant that it was more legend than history. Why now after all of these years? What had changed? Why had the Terrans left the protective womb of their gravity well to go chasing after their long-lost prodigal children?

Mitchell shook his head as if to clear it. As a Special High+, we was among the top one percent of his kind: a savant by the standards of those with Down syndrome, much like the ancient pioneer who'd given his name to the ship that had carried him between worlds. Which he knew made him something like a very clever twelve-year-old. He was way out of his depth trying to second guess the ancient, decadent, and nearly legendary government of Earth.

They arrived at the edge of the Manyatta: a vast, circus tent sized structure of lead impregnated organic nanoweave. Inflated with breathable air, it was the portable home of Sironka's clan. A group of Maasai emerged to escort the anti-grav platforms to mate with reticules that emerged like flailing anemone from its sides. The two of them entered through more traditional airlock. Safely inside, they were able to remove their protective gear; or, in Mitchell's case, retract the dome which normally sheltered his head beneath its transparent embrace. The rest of his environmental gear simply deflated and shrunk down to become a brightly colored jumpsuit. Sironka pulled his ragtag rig apart piece-by-piece, revealing a dark-skinned, intelligent-looking man roughly Mitchell's own age. Like most of the Maasai, Mitchell found him to be impossibly tall, thin, and handsome. They were also athletic, with none of the cherubic chubbiness typical of the Downstar's inhabitants.

"Welcome home Mitchell Green," he rumbled in his kettledrum-low voice. "Welcome to the Manyatta of the Maasai!" The huts were circular and mud colored, with corrals containing goats, chickens, and sheep. But they were constructed of molecule-thin smart fabric that could be collapsed into one meter cubes and then re-erected with a mild electrical charge. And clean, very clean. Even the animal's dung was collected down to the grain and reused as fertilizer.

Not that Mitchell was unfamiliar with these ideas. He was a lifelong station dweller, after all. Nothing was ever wasted. Nothing. At a station it was even worse, in fact. A planet is filled with stuff. On a station there is simply no more stuff.

Sironka and Special made their way to the center of the Manyatta. As was traditional when the Maasai received a pilot from the Downstar, a banquet had been carefully planned. In fact, it was already underway so that the Special wouldn't feel embarrassed by too much attention. Even though the feast was in his honor, Mitchell's presence was acknowledged by little more than a friendly cheer from the gathered Maasai.

Which was exactly how he liked it. It was like always coming home.

He took his seat next to the clan doctor – again as was traditional for a guest. In Martian Maasai culture, the Doctor was the *de facto* leader, revered even above other such senior figures as its Chieftain, Lead Scientist, and Midwife. He was also the only member of the clan to possess Sentience. Mitchell could somehow sense his companion machine exchanging greetings – "shaking hands" in the parlance of their kind – with that of the Doctor's.

The gray-haired man peered down at him with a bemused expression.

"So Traveler, you've joined us once again?"

Mitchell smiled back in response, nodding. The Doctor didn't really expect an answer. Mitchell sat down on an ornate blanket next to the older man, crossing his legs carefully. Together they watched the clan's young people perform the *adumu,* or jumping dance. They leapt high into the air, their shuka swirling about their long bodies, joyfully competing with one another to see who could fling themselves hardest against the weak pull of Mar's gravity. They formed a circle, with one or two at a time in the center, arms pressed tightly against their sides, heady thrown back, heels never touching the ground. The pitch of their voices rose and fell based on the height of the jump.

"Mitchell," Sentience spoke quietly into his earbud. "The clan Sentience isn't at all happy about the Posthegemony probe being destroyed. Neither was the Doctor. But they were visiting another clan's manyatta and weren't able to intervene."

"What's the problem exactly?" he sub-vocalized in response, not wanting to offend his hosts. He thought he knew the answer already, but he wanted to hear it from Sentience. Perhaps if he didn't actually conceptualize the truth it would somehow pass by his friends, leaving them alone to continue their lives uninterrupted, like the shadow of one of Mars' few clouds passing quickly over the russet oceans of grass.

"The problem dear boy is that the Posthegemony is not only arrogant, but vengeful." Sentience always sounded pedantic to Mitchell. Like an impatient teacher or something. But he put up with it, because that was the way it had always been. Annoying. "Sentience is afraid of their response. It's in all of the ancient history records. They always make examples of those who defy them. *Always.*"

"What can we do about it?" Mitchell already knew and dreaded the answer. Sentience didn't respond. Which he knew was an answer in and of itself. Nothing.

Now Sironka was among the dancers, flinging his body joyfully upward alongside his friends, the other men and women of his age set. Brothers and sisters, Mitchell supposed, in a very real sense. Higher and higher he leapt, his laughter audible above the rising and falling voices of the other Maasai, a vision of everything Mitchell could never be: agile, tall, dark, and heroic.

Then their world exploded.

Nadine Mang: Antichthon, Downstar Station

It wasn't the reception Captain Nadine Shu Tun Mang had expected.

When the brief disorientation caused by the materialization of her hologram ended, she didn't as usual find herself "standing" in the cheerful, slightly dingy corridors of the Downstar Station, surrounded by retarded children and doddering elders. Instead, she found herself upended into the center of what appeared to be a massive three-sided table, the normally diminutive form of Cassidy Brazo looming above her like some sort of primordial Greek titan, scowls and wrath darkening her flawed features.

It was... disconcerting.

Nadine quickly turned to examine the other two sides of the table. On one side a tired-looking Hispanic man leaned back in an ancient office chair, his eyes melancholy. The other was occupied by a Downstar Sentience, it's normally comically bright display a barrage of deep, angry reds.

"Ah," she folded her arms in a gesture of impatience. "The Triumvirate, I presume? What is the meaning of this?" It was the first lesson they taught at Producer-Consumer's Army Space Command officer's school: when dealing with primitives, always assume an aura of superiority.

"You presume correctly Captain Mang," the Sentience's synthesized voice matched her own for condescension. "You should feel privileged to be allowed to project your consciousness anywhere onto Downstar Station at this time."

"Really?" she feigned ignorance. "And why would that be? Do you normally treat visitors this way?"

"We don't normally have visitors." the Hispanic man leaned forward, starting at her with surprisingly perceptive eyes. "And we've never had one that attacked Mars while visiting us. Would you mind explaining that *mi amiga?*"

His voice was surprisingly mild. Cassidy's was not.

"You attacked the Maasai!" she sputtered furiously, "And you did it while my fiancé was visiting them. And *you knew that he was visiting them!*"

"We did no such thing." She responded calmly. *Shit,* she thought to herself. *They must have intercepted the broadcast from that idiot satellite we left in orbit around the planet.* "They attacked us, and our communications satellite automatically responded in self-defense. And it did so completely without my authorization. However, it responded with non-lethal force. I'm certain your fiancé is fine Ms. Brazo."

"What did they attack it with? Ping pong balls?" Brazo hissed.

"Why would a 'medical vessel' need to carry weapons at all, lethal or not?" the man interrupted, sounding far too reasonable. "Furthermore, we know that the satellite you left in orbit around Mars contained both a military AI and specialized nanotechnology weapons. How could we not? It was eager to tell anyone who would listen. Not exactly the sort of behavior one would expect from someone dedicated to 'reaching out to all of the Earth's lost children,' as I believe you put it."

"Unless you're reaching out to hit them," Cassidy added angrily. Surprisingly to Nadine, neither of her fellow triumvirs – the two smart ones – made any motion to correct her.

"We really know very little about you. Any of you," she responded smoothly. Nadine realized that she had to regain control of the conversation. "Yes, we knew the Maasai had settled on Mars. And we knew from our ancient histories that they were and, as it turned out, still are an aggressive, warlike people. We sent them a peaceful embassy, just as we sent you one to you. Unlike you, they attacked. We responded."

"Why?" asked the Downstar Sentience.

"Why what?" she was genuinely confused.

"Why did you need to respond?" it continued. "Why not just leave them alone? Surely you could have opened trade with one of the other Martian settlements. Some of them are pacifists. Why pick a group you knew to be warlike in the first place?"

"They were the only one we were aware of."

"I calculate that to be highly unlikely," it snipped back at her. "In fact, the answer is quite simple. You wanted to make an example out of someone to establish your superiority."

"We don't have to 'establish' our superiority!" she snapped back, instantly regretting it. Silence fell. *Like the grave,* she thought. It lasted far too long, seemingly echoing around what to her appeared to be the vast chamber on wings of finality.

"You attacked our allies the Maasai," Cassidy eventually said, speaking slowly so there could be no misunderstanding her. "And you did it while Mitchell was there. Our ambassador..."

"Cassidy, people like you don't have 'allies' and 'ambassadors'," she interrupted. The words were bursting out of her now, condescending, uncontrolled, and honest. It was the wrong thing to do. She knew that. But she let her anger flair anyway. What did it matter? What could they do? How dare these primitives, these quasi-humans question her! "You aren't countries or nations. You aren't peoples. Such things haven't existed in a millennium, and they will never exist again. You're just... sick people. You and the others like you most especially Cassidy. You know that. All of you Interesting People are just children that wandered too far away from their parents, got lost, and forgot to grow up. Like millions and millions of Peter Pans and Wendys from a fairy tale. Surely none of you thought that you could get away with it forever? Sooner or later, everyone has to give up their fantasies, wake from their dreams, and grow up."

The Special and her Standard friend simply stared at her. She imagined that the Sentience was staring as well, though there was no way to tell.

"Look," she tried again, regaining control of herself. "The Earth is reaching out to you. We want to help you people — all of you, including the Maasai. Take our hand and we will lift you up to heights none of you have ever imagined possible. You'll live without sickness and for so long that you'll be practically immortal. Your bodies will be beautiful, powerful, and young. None of you will ever have to go hungry again. All of the entertainment of a millennium of human civilization will be at your fingertips. All we want is for you people to agree to evolve! It's for your own good."

"And the Devil took him up into an exceedingly high mountain, and showed him all the kingdoms of the world, and the glory of them;" the Hispanic triumvir's voice was sad, slow, and full of resignation. "And he said to him: 'All of these things I give you, if you will but bow down and worship me.'"

"We aren't devils!" she snapped confusedly, completely missing the reference. "We aren't tempting you with glory and we don't want your worship. All we want to do is to draw all of you back into the family of humanity before its too late. Look at her and that ridiculous Sentience! *Look at them!*"

She gestured up at Cassidy and the machine intelligence with her tiny holographic arms, and then turned her eyes up to the Standard triumvir.

"You're devolving due to isolation, genetic disease, and technological backwardness. And the Maasai are worse than you people. Look at them: they're barely human at this point!"

Cassidy Brazo's face glared down at her, large as a moon, her mongoloid features alien and incomprehensible. The Terran captain couldn't tell if she was angry, confused, disappointed, or some baffling combination of all three. Her mouth hung open, showing off a segment of her oversized tongue.

"It isn't the Maasai who are barely human at this point," she said at last. And, stabbing downward with one of her stubby fingers, she severed the connection. Then, looking defiantly at the other two triumvirs, she added: "The 21st chromosome. It's where they keep all the awesome."

Cassidy Brazo: Antichthon, Downstar Station

"Okay, so now we really are at war with the Earth." Sentience sounded more relieved than exasperated, though its tone of voice managed to convey both. "Since we don't have any weapons, what do you two clever organics propose we do?"

"We run away." Cassidy said simply. Pablo Livni nodded his head thoughtfully in agreement.

"Our AntiG engines are fully functional and our fuel tanks are full," he added. "We used them less than an Earth standard year ago to fix a problem with our orbit. We could definitely flee. In fact, we might even be faster than the *Asclepius* despite her modernity and smaller mass. Our ancestors fitted big, big engines into the scraper that eventually became the Station. They might not be up-to-date, but they're huge and they're powerful."

Downstar Station was positioned in a roughly antichthon counter-Earth orbit on precisely the opposite side of the Sun. It wasn't really invisible, of course. Even S.A.C era technology would have been capable of detecting it using coronagraphs. It's position was more of a gesture by the inhabitants of the station; a perpetual way of saying "leave us alone" or possibly "screw you." And, of course, out of sight was generally out of mind as well. At least until now.

"Alright," agreed Sentience after a brief pause, "the Master AI and I agree at least tentatively, based on the data we've gathered so far observing the *Asclepius*. Where do you want to flee too, then?"

"Dihya." Cassidy answered firmly. "Queen Dihya. We go to the *Imazighen* in the Belt."

Pablo chewed on his stylus.

"The Berbers on 4 Vesta... why them, Cassidy?"

"They have big ships, big guns, and bad attitudes." She paused thoughtfully, and then followed with, "They'll use them, too. We can head toward them. If the Terrans follow us, they'll attack. They hate the Terrans."

He nodded in agreement.

"Then I think it's time to let everyone in the system know everything that we know. Sentience?"

"Wait." Cassidy looked thoughtful. "What do we know, really? We know what their AI broadcast, but that's it. Can we talk to Mitchell? The *Andrew Levitz?*"

"Not yet." Sentience sounded thoughtful. "Arabia Terra is on the opposite side of the planet from us right now – and there aren't any communication satellites we're aware of in orbit around Mars. It'll be another six hours before we can communicate with them by tightbeam."

"Then we start running now," the little Special sounded unusually certain. "But when we are able to reach Mitchell or his ship, we broadcast what they tell us on broadbeam to everyone. Every child of the Nakba needs to know that they've done on Mars. And what they said to us."

They are all silent once again. Finally, with the electronic equivalent of a sigh, Sentience spoke. "If we do that, the master AI and I calculate there is a 91.2% likelihood that the human race will be plunged into a civil war of vast and unprecedented proportions. We also calculate..."

It actually hesitated. But only for a few, brief seconds.

"...we calculate that we will lose that war. Definitively."

It didn't provide a statistic.

"Doesn't matter," she responded. "We're already at war with them."

"She's right." Pablo added. "When you think about it, we've been at war for over a thousand years now. One we didn't want and didn't start. One that drove us from our ancestral homes, and then scattered us like dust into the depths of space. It's just that they forgot about us for a while. Or lost interest. Who knows? It's hardly important now. What matters is that we can either fight or run."

"We run now," said Cassidy firmly. "Then later, we fight."

Mitchell Green: Mars, Arabia Terra

Mitchell had always hated his earbud. Though it was supposed to be custom shaped for his ear, it never felt right. It was irritating and uncomfortable. It gave him tiny rashes.. He wasn't supposed to be able to feel it, either. But he could.

It also meant that Sentience and the *Andrew Levitz's* AI could chatter to one another right inside of his head. Which was extremely annoying and unwelcome. Except that this time, it wasn't.

"Wake up wake up wake up wake up wake up wake up..." It didn't sound like his Sentience at all. More like one of the alarm claxons that went off on the station when something started to depressurize. He tried to ignore it, but couldn't. It sounded like a drum machine going off inside of his brain.

"Alright, all right! Just make it stop." He levered himself groggily up, resting on his elbows. For some reason his suit had deployed, inflating itself. His dome-like helmet was in place and he was breathing canned air. His vision was too blurry to make out details. For a few moments he couldn't remember where he was. He wasn't even sure who he was.

Sentience was talking. Yelling, actually. He tried hard to focus.

"...depressurizing the Manyatta!" it shrieked. Could a machine panic? "Pressure at 73% and declining! Nanoweave unable to deploy around the breach; it's too large!"

Suddenly everything came into focus.

The Maasai lay scattered about their village like broken dolls. Their homes had suffered surprisingly little damage; only those close to the epicenter of the impact had been flattened. But the atmosphere of the Manyatta was escaping. Mitchell could see it go: a vague plume of white against the russet of the Martian sky.

He stood up quickly.

"What do I do?" he implored, detesting he panicky, whining quality of his own voice. "We have to make it stop!"

"The Doctor's Sentience says that there is a repair kit at the base of the wall." His Sentience answered. It sounded breathless; a physical impossibility, but there it was. "You have to get it, and scale up the wall to where the hole is. The Manyatta AI will help you by manipulating the nanoweave, and I'm going to project a map inside of your helmet. But hurry!"

A compass-like diagram dominated by a large, red arrow appeared suddenly before his eyes. Mitchell scrambled to follow it, tripping over fallen Maasai, panicked chickens freed by the explosion, and shattered bits of hut as he made his way toward the inner wall of the huge structure. After a seeming eternity he reached it and, after working his way around a goat pen and what looked like a small water purification plant, found a backpack mounted directly to its surface. It came away immediately when he grabbed it, almost as if the wall itself was thrusting it at him.

"Pressure at 67 percent! We have to fix that leak Mitchell!"

The young Special looked around blankly, not really understanding.

"But how do I get up there?" he pleaded. "There's no ladder or anything!"

"Just start climbing! The AI will take care of everything."

"Okay." Mitchell reached out and touched the wall. It grabbed him. With a yelp he reflexively yanked his hand back. Then, steadying himself, he reached out again. The nanoweave surface wrapped itself around his gloved hand, holding him firmly. He reached up with his other hand with the same result. He followed with one boot, then the other. Before he knew it Mitchell was scaling up the wall, the artificial assistance and weak Martian gravity giving him an unaccustomed sensation of incredible strength. It would have been fun if the situation hadn't been so desperate.

"Pressure at 64 percent! You have to hurry!"

Before very long Mitchell found himself upside-down above the village of the Maasai, moving hand-over-hand toward the gaping wound in the center of the Manyatta's protective wall. He shivered with fear. It wasn't like working in a vacuum. If the wall failed to grip his limbs he would tumble to the ground far below. Furthermore, he could increasingly feel the hard, cold pull of the atmosphere breach upon his body. Soon, if the wall failed him, he would be pulled through the gap and flung high into the air to tumble to the ground below. In the weak Martian atmosphere he would probably survive a fall straight down. But he wouldn't survive being sucked through that hole.

He was close now, the escaping air like a hurricane around him. He could see the hole clearly, and was surprised to see that it was perfectly circular and roughly the size of a large table. He'd expected something larger and more ragged. Then he remembered the nanoweave wall holding his hands and feet. The Manyatta AI had desperately attempted to close the tear left by the... well, Mitchell didn't know what it was exactly. A Posthegemony missile, perhaps? But it simply hadn't had the flexibility or raw mass to close it all the way.

"Pressure at 59%!"

"What do I do?" Mitchell asked, sounding surprisingly calm even to himself. He was frightened but, like any spacer that survived childhood, he knew how to contain and compartmentalize his fears during emergency situations. He'd been trained from an early age to know how. It some ways it was little different for him than a 21st Century person dealing with their car breaking down at night on an isolated and unfamiliar road. Scary, upsetting, and potentially dangerous, but most likely everything would turn out okay.

"Open the backpack, remove the contents, and throw them at the opening. Quickly, Mitchell!"

Idly he wondered how well his Sentience would survive being sucked through the breach and hurled several hundred meters to the ground along with him. *Probably just fine,* he thought sourly. Being made out of hardened plasteel and quantum circuitry had a lot of advantages.

Nevertheless, the young Special took a deep breath and let go with both of his hands, trusting the Manyatta AI to hold onto his feet. It did. Which didn't keep him from being blown desperately about like a leaf in the wind which he struggled to remove the contents of the backpack. He caught a brief glimpse of something that like looked like a folded silver emergency blanket and then it was gone, torn from his grasp. However, the instant it left his hand, the "blanket" unfolded into a large, rigid square of nanoweave at least five times larger than the diameter of the puncture. The pull of the vacuum sucked it straight into the hole, covering it, and a moment later the silver square was busily interlacing itself into the fabric of the nanoweave wall.

"Atmosphere breach contained," Sentience said with obvious relief. Perhaps it hadn't been eager to test the hypothetical limits of its hardening, Mitchell thought. "Manyatta atmosphere repressurizing. You saved them Mitchell. You saved everyone here."

He sighed with relief. He was a hero! And then he realized that he was hanging upside-down fifty meters above the ground.

It was a slow, careful crawl back down to the Maasai village. Once the excitement of the moment had worn off, Mitchell found that he felt dizzy and more than a little queasy. Not at all like a hero. He just felt sick. And what he found when he finally made it to the ground didn't make him feel any better.

None of the Maasai had woken up. He slowly and carefully made his way through the village, back to where the festival had been. They all lay where they had fallen, as if they were puppets whose strings had been suddenly and artlessly cut. He found the Doctor sprawled out on the ornate rug where the two of them had sat for the *adumu,* his long dark limbs splayed at uncomfortable angles. Mitchell arranged him into a more comfortable position, and then sat down next to him, his head in his hands. He felt like crying. But he forced the sobs back down into his gut, knowing that he was a captain and thus couldn't break down in the midst of crisis.

"Are they all dead?" He asked Sentience after a few stolen moments of silence, not really wanting to know the answer.

"No," it responded quickly. "No one seems to have been injured in the attack. But they are all in comas and, if we can't do something about it quickly, they could die of dehydration."

Mitchell gestured at the Doctor's Sentience: a small, yellow and brown disk which hung from his throat by leather cords.

"What does it think?"

"I have been comparing notes with the Manyatta AI and the Doctor's Sentience since the attack. We know that the coma is deliberate and medical in nature. The artificial viruses at work in their systems have rendered them unconscious while they do their work. We are not certain what that work is exactly, but we believe that there are changes taking place on a genetic level."

"Artificial viruses?" Mitchell asked, a little confused.

"Nanotechnology, really. Tiny machines smaller than cells that reprogram the body. We don't make them anymore." Sentience paused for a moment. "These are very advanced; far beyond anything in my pre-Nakba records, or anything that the Maasai use."

"Those are the things we fled Earth to get away from, right? The things that could erase our minds?" Mitchell knew at least hypothetically what nanotechnology was. But he didn't really understand what it could do.

"In part yes," replied Sentience. After a pause. "Or at least that was what your ancestors believed."

"Do any of the Interesting People on Mars know anything more about them? Or are there any really good doctors on Mars?"

Sentience paused fractionally, which Mitchell knew meant he was talking to the other computer intelligences.

"Our best bet is to travel to Monique Wittag Colony in the Martian arctic region. There are some others, but they either aren't well known to the Maasai or are too far away."

"Who lives there?" asked Mitchell curiously.

"They are the people who you referred to as 'feminists' in your conversation with Sironka. Though that isn't a particularly accurate description. A better one would be that they are sister-clones of a Francophone separatist lesb..."

"Sironka!" Mitchell yelped, rising to his feet. He ran to the circle where the *adumu* dancers lay limply together like a pile of children's dolls. He carefully rolled them apart one-by-one, only stopping when he found his friend: unconscious, mouth open, and stripped of his dignity. Guilt shot through him, a hot and wet river of emotion. He'd been so overwhelmed by the slowly unfolding apocalypse around him that he'd forgotten his friend.

And then he did weep.

🚀 🚀 🚀

It took Mitchell a while to recover from his crying. He thought he would never, ever stop. He was dehydrated and dry-sniffling by the time he was done. And it was extremely humiliating, what with him being a captain and all. But the Sentiences and Manyatta AIs kept silent throughout the entire episode. Possibly they understood.

More likely they did not. But they kept respectfully silent all the same.

Mitchell laid his friend out on the ground as comfortably as he could possibly manage. He spent the next few hours wandering through the Manyatta, doing the same for every Maasai man, woman, and child he could find. If comforted him to see them looking comfortable. When he was both exhausted and relatively certain he'd found every lat one, he summoned the *Andrew Levitz* to come pick him up with two words.

"Come here."

A few moments later a vast, oblong shape with stubby wings hovered above the Maasai dwelling, casting its long shadow across the scene of tragedy below. It was impressive. And it was his. But Mitchell's shoulder's sagged. He no longer felt anything like a hero. Instead, he felt like what he was: a small, weak, and simple man with a learning disability for whom life had just become very, very complicated.

Still, he was a captain. And he had a job to do.

🚀 🚀 🚀

They flew north. The usual chatter between Sentience and AI was muted, the two machine intelligences were respecting his desire for silence within the limits of their abilities. Mitchell was lost in thought. The events of the proceeding day were all jumbled up inside of him, a storm of worry and horror. What had the Earthers done to them? Could he make it better? Would his act of heroism even matter if he couldn't wake them up? And finally: were the Children of the Nakba at war with the Earth?

These dark thoughts were interrupted by all of the ship's alarms going off.

"We're under fire!" screamed the ship's AI, its artificial voice high with panic. "S.A.C. era Gauss rifle firing depleted uranium spheres! They just fired a warning shot thirty meters off of our port side."

"The Monique Wittag Colony AI is signaling us." Sentience spoke at the same time, the machines' voices interrupting and overlapping one another. Fortunately, Mitchell had what felt like a lifetime's worth of practice listening to this kind of mechanical babble. "They're demanding we identify ourselves or be blown from the sky."

"Just tell them what just happened," he said grimly. "That should do it."

There was a brief pause.

"The colony AI says that we should land on the ice two kilometers away. They will send representatives to speak with us."

Mitchell nodded his ascent. A moment later the ship landed on the trackless Martian ice with a slight jolt. He waited in silence, save for the occasional background chatter between the two machine intelligences and their counterpart in the colony.

"Tracked vehicle approaching," the AI stated after a while. It sounded much calmer now. "Moving at approximately 40 kilometers per Earth standard hour. Vehicle AI signaling us. It contains three passengers who identify themselves as medical personnel."

He peered at the approaching vehicle using several of the ship's external cameras. It was a battered, ancient-looking device, obviously designed to move across the frozen surfaces of Mars' poles. It also didn't look particularly threatening. So he signaled the ship's AI to open the airlock for them.

Five minutes later he was sharing the cramped cabin of the *Andrew Levitz* with three brunet women his own height. There were as far as he could tell identical, with bobbed boyish hair and slightly aquiline noses. They wore tattered turtleneck sweaters, short skirts, berets, high boots, and stood as far away as they could possibly get from him without actually leaving the room, staring at Mitchell through enormous dark eyes. They clutched what he assumed were medical bags with nervous, slender fingers.

"Hello," he said simply. "I'm Captain Mitchell Green. What are your names?"

"You may call us Un, Deux, and Trois." They looked so much alike that he honestly couldn't tell which one of them had said it. Maybe Deux? And their accents were so strange that he could barely understand their Spanglanese. But he persevered.

"So you're doctors? You'll be able to help the Maasai?" he asked hopefully.

"*Oui* – we are scientists with medical training." This time Mitchell really wasn't sure which one had spoken. "Whether or not we can help them, we do not know yet. *On verra bien.*"

Her hand fluttered uncertainly.

"Well then." Mitchell felt flustered. He found the three women extremely unsettling, but didn't want to offend them. In fact, he desperately needed them if he was going to save Sironka, the Doctor, and the other Maasai. And he really didn't know very much about them. Maybe this was this way of being friendly.

"Well then," he repeated, "you can pull down seats from the wall behind you. There are safety belts too, if you want to strap in. But the ride should be pretty smooth unless we hit some kind of storm."

One of the woman (Was it Un?) shook her head uncomfortably, gesturing with her hand.

"We will stand, unless an emergency it becomes."

"Okay." Mitchell busied himself with the controls – though this was mostly for show so that he could stop staring at his passengers. The AI had as always been listening for a verbal cue, and would handle most of the work. The Andrew *Levitz slowly rose into the air, and then shot southward back toward the Manyatta.*

"You know," Sentience told him conspiratorially, "none of these clones has ever seen a man before outside of pictures and holograms. You're the first one they've seen in person."

"Really?" he turned to the three women, who were whispering among themselves in a language he didn't understand. He had no idea what a clone was. "Am I the first man you've ever seen?"

"Mitchell!" hissed Sentience in shocked annoyance. It even said it out loud for once, rather than through his earbud.

The three of them looked at him with expressions that ranged from puzzlement to alarm. The cabin grew very, very silent.

"Oui – there are no men in our colony," replied the one he thought was called Trois at last. He detected what might have been panic in her voice. "Outside of viewing historical records, you are the first."

"Oh." Mitchell scratched his spiky red hair thoughtfully. He really needed a bath. "Okay. That must have made it hard dealing with the Maasai, though."

"Non. We always dealt with woman of that tribe, usually the one they called the Midwife. Never with their men."

"Oh." He hadn't thought of that. "You'll help the men as well as the women, though, right? I mean, they all need your help right now: men, women, and kids. All of them."

The three looked at one another.

"Oui." The one he had decided to call Trois answered. "We will help everyone equally."

Mitchell nodded and returned to his controls. Though there was not much for him to do, he *was* the captain. These three strange women were his responsibility, and he intended to keep an eye on the external cameras for any more signs of attack. From what Sentience had told him on the trip out the Earther attack hadn't been an explosive. It hadn't been designed to destroy a ship or anything like that. But that didn't mean they *didn't* have a weapon like that, did it?

It was a silent flight back to the Manyatta, everyone locked away inside of their own thoughts. Mitchell simply wanted his friends to wake up. The Maasai were superheroes as far as he was concerned. Once they were awake, they would know what to do about everything. He was certain of it.

What his three odd passengers were thinking was a mystery to him. What the machines thought wasn't. As always, they chattered away to one another inside of his ear.

And, as always, it was annoying and not very interesting.

The *Andrew Levitz* settled down on the tall russet grass next to the towering walls of the Manyatta, odd Martian cattle scattering in its wake. The women retreated to the airlock to don their pressure suits: patched, ancient-looking gear with fishbowl helmets. When they were finished he joined them, his colorful safety suit deploying around him automatically.

"We must all keep our suits on until I say, *non?*" Trois (he decided) tapped her helmet. "What they have might be contagious, though I doubt it. Still..."

She gave an odd little shrug. Mitchell nodded. He hadn't retracted his helmet last time, either. But that was because he'd been first so terrified – and then so horrified – that he'd forgotten.

As he had what seemed like an eternity before, Mitchell and Un-Deux-Trois moved through the whispering field toward the smoothly curved pressure wall of the Maasai village. Only this time there were no cheerful young men to greet them outside of its protective perimeter. Instead there was only silence.

The Manyatta AI cycled the airlock for them and they passed within. The village was quite save for the braying of goats and the familiar, almost imperceptible whoosh, whoosh of air recyclers. The Maasai lay where Mitchell had arranged them in neat rows like so many dolls in a shop window.

The guided the three women through the village to where the Doctor lay. They were wide eyed behind their fishbowls, desperately trying to look in every direction at once, their expressions both curious and alarmed. Mitchell guessed that their colony wasn't much like this one. Finally they wove their way through slumbering villagers to the center square. Mitchell regretfully led them past the row of dancers to where the Doctor lay, looking distinguished and serene despite his state.

"He's there leader," Mitchell explained, "His Sentience is talking to mine. Should you like, it will talk with you and your medical gear as well."

It was an overly simplistic way of explaining what would happen. In the way of his kind, the Special had more problems saying things than actually thinking them. Nevertheless, Un-Deux-Trois nodded simultaneously. Then, glancing at one another, two of them began removing various devices from their bag, while the third looked at him appraising.

"That would be good Captain – very helpful." She responded a bit haltingly, "Very thoughtful."

Of course Mitchell didn't really have to "do" anything. He knew that the various Sentiences and AIs were listening to everything they said, while simultaneously gabbing back and forth at incomprehensible speeds in the way of their kind. He could listen to it should he wish; a song of half-understood words, screeches, and chirps. But he didn't wish.

Then for the first time it occurred to him that the women didn't seem to be accustomed to interacting with machine intelligences. This struck him as extremely odd. While Mars wasn't as extreme an environment as space, it was still a very hostile one, requiring extensive technological assistance. And he knew that their colony had its own AI... though what that meant precisely he didn't know. There were many classes of machine intelligence. Every spacer knew that the AI in his suit wasn't in the same league as the AI on the *Andrew Levitz* (or any other ship), which wasn't even in the same league as Sentience. Was their colony AI more like the one in his suit, then? Or was it more a matter of culture? It struck Mitchell that the gulf between himself and the three nervous women may be even greater the one between himself and the Maasai.

Was it even crossable? He hoped so. If there was going to be a war, it would have to be. He didn't think the Posthegemony would see much difference between the Children of the Nakba, even if those differences seemed dramatic to the Children themselves.

Mitchell wandered over to where Sironka lay. The young man didn't seem to be in any particular distress; though is eyes fluttered slightly, as if he were dreaming. His features were serene; his brow, cool. The Special leveled himself onto the ground with a sigh. Events were moving rapidly past him – too rapidly to be grasped completely. For Mitchell life was a leisurely stroll down a flowered path, not a rough jog around a track. His mind couldn't be rushed. So he had a hard time imagining what a war with the Earth would be like, or even why anyone would want to fight one. He couldn't really fathom what had been done to the Maasai, either. Only that it had been bad, and that it had to be undone.

He wasn't certain how long he had sat on the russet-colored Martian grass, letting his thoughts take their leisurely course. A while certainly. He thought about Cassidy and his upcoming wedding. He thought about his home. In fact, he began to get a bit homesick. It was an unfamiliar emotion. Mitchell liked traveling, even though until now those travels had consisted entirely of going between the Downstar and Arabia Terra. He enjoyed having the title Captain, even while understanding that it was mostly an honorarium, because it meant that he was one of the few of his kind that would ever travel.

Sentience interrupted his thoughts.

"Sappho, Gertrude Stein, and Alice B. Toklas are going to try and wake up the doctor now," it said in a mocking tone of voice that Mitchell found entirely inappropriate, even if he didn't understand it. "His Sentience and the Manyatta AI would *very* much prefer it if you were there when they did it, too."

"Are those really their names?" he asked, confused.

"No," it replied quickly. Another one of its odd pauses followed. "And please forget I said anything."

Baffled, Mitchell wandered back to where the three women hovered over the long, prone form of the Doctor. Curiously, they'd removed their ancient pressure suits. He pointed at them and shrugged questioningly.

"It isn't contagious Captain." He'd more-or-less given up attempting to figure out which woman was which by this time, preferring to think of them as Un-Deux-Trois: a single individual. "Or, at least, we do not believe it is contagious to us. To others like this one..."

She gestured down at the Doctor.

"...it is very likely *extremely* contagious."

He nodded, not really knowing what else to do.

"We shall now wake him up with a shot of high intensity Modafinil," she said. "We have a theory about what the nanovirus has done to his physiology, but cannot be sure until he is awake, *non?"*

"And that theory is what, exactly?" interjected his Sentience.

The three of them exchanged yet another one of their maddening glances before shrugging at once.

"It is best not to say yet. It is, at this point, pure speculation." Un-Deux-Trois waved her hand dismissively. "We shall know shortly in any case."

Mitchell nodded slowly, again not really knowing what to make of the woman's alien glances and gestures. They seemed to be waiting for his permission to proceed. It struck him for the first time that Un-Deux-Trois had no idea he was a Special. This seemed crazy (he looked very much like one after all), until he remembered that they had never actually seen a man before, either. And, really, were his small stature, flat features, and epicanthic folds any more alien to them than the towering height, dark skin, and alien thinness of the Maasai? The women of this sequestered, strange culture had withdrawn not only from the Earth, but from all contact with opposite sex. Which, effectively, put them out of contact with practically everyone. Like himself, they probably had only a vague concept of the complexities of the outside world.

Yet their foremothers had arrived on Mars by ship; a ship which undoubtedly had had a captain of its own. Respect for this rank was a universal constant among the Children of the Nakba. Captains were the saviors of nations and the deliverers of peoples. So he'd introduced himself as The Captain, and they'd taken him at his word. He was in charge by dint of tradition and folklore. It was no more complex than that.

Un-Deux-Trois was still looking at him expectantly.

"Yes, please," he said at last. "Wake him up. He's very wise and a doctor like you are. He can help."

Without further comment she pressed something that looked very much like a gun against the neck of the Maasai elder. There was a brief hissing sound. A moment later the Doctor began shaking uncontrollably. His eyes opened, and rolled wildly about, straining to see everything at once. Finally, he tried to lever himself upright, but failed. Mitchell knelled down next to him and gave him some water. The three women kept their distance.

The old man tried to speak, but his words were slurred and difficult. After a few moments he gave up and began sub-vocalizing to his Sentience instead.

"Traveler I see that you have returned yet again," it translated. After a moment, "And Sentience tells me that you saved us as well. And that you've brought friends to help us."

"I'm not sure they're friends," he answered ruefully, glancing up at his companions. "But they agreed to help. Can you tell us what's wrong?"

"I'm very weak." He managed to roll his head so that he faced Mitchell. "Like a baby. No muscle tone. Or like a man that has been in a coma for a long time. How long have I been unconscious?"

"Not that long. Maybe half an Earth day."

The Doctor was silent for a while. He looked up at the women. His sentience spoke for him, it's speakers recreating his rich, baritone voice.

"Then this would be our 'example' from the Posthegemony, would it not sisters? Genetic hypotonia?"

It wasn't really a question. Un-Deux-Trois nodded all at once.

"*Oui.* Extremely severe. Also, there is an airborne viral component which makes it contagious to all who share your genotype – though it should be harmless to all else. It is most likely hereditary as well."

Mitchell sat down hard, pulling his knees to his chest. He placed his head between his palms and stared at the ground, rubbing his temples with his index fingers.

"The Traveler has some passing familiarity with this disorder, I think." His tone was mildly ironic, but Mitchell simply nodded. He had it himself of course, though his hypotonia was comparatively mild. He exercised fanatically, stayed away from sweets, and took muscle building drugs. He was also lucky. He was somewhat weak compared to an average S.A.C. era male, but still statistically within the spectrum of normal for a spacer. But others....

"Is it correctable?" the Maasai elder's tone was mild, almost disinterested. As if he were discussing an abstract problem. Or possibly Sentience was translating his tone incorrectly, though Mitchell doubted it. "We could use tailored nanobots to conduct chromosomal reprogramming? Or perhaps rebuild muscle tone using an implanted stimulus net?"

Un-Deux-Trois shook her head.

"*Non.* The artificial viruses they've introduced into your system will combat all of these things. The technology is quite advanced; beyond anything that we possess, or even thought to be possible. It is very, very sophisticated. Multi-functioning. Possibly with a limited collective AI. We suspect that, if pressed, it will attack the host body. Most likely the nervous system."

"So if we fight it, we die. And if we don't, we also die." he responded grimly.

"No." Mitchell shook his head, surprised by his own boldness. "It can be lived with. On the Downstar we have places the size of your village set aside. The AntiG is very low in them. We can teach you how to live with it. Some of us live our whole lives that way."

But even as he spoke the words, Mitchell knew them to be hopeless. How could they live like Specials: handicapped, physically restricted, trapped indoors in small spaces? Weak and helpless in normal gravity for their entire lives? He couldn't imagine the leaping, vigorous Sironka living that way. Or the Doctor, Midwife, and countless other Maasai he knew. They were too bold, too virile. They were warriors and cowboys, not Specials. They simply wouldn't do it.

"And risk spreading the disease to others?" the Doctor replied gently. "If it spread to the other Manyatta, it could destroy all Maasai, rather than just one tribe. Better to lose a single hand than to poison the whole body."

"I could take all of you off the planet in the *Andrew Levitz*." He tried again. "The ship's cabin can't hold all of you, but the containers are airtight. We can rig breathing lines to them. It should be safe enough so long as we don't get caught in a solar flare. Then we can make for the Downstar; or, if you like, for the Belt. We know the Imazighen and burako-extropian enclaves. They know how to make stations out of asteroids. They helped my ancestors make one. You'll never come into contact with other Maasai out there."

The Doctor shook his head sadly.

"We are people of the red land. Of cattle and long grasses. Of Earth once, and now of Mars. We cannot live in such a way. We cannot live weak and disgraced. Better to die here. Better that my people slumber eternally having never awoken."

"And what about us? All of us?" Much to his surprise Mitchell found himself growing angry; an extreme social blunder among his own kind. He stood quickly, almost losing his balance. He clenched and unclenched his gloved hands, fighting for self-control. "We don't know how to fight a war. You-"

He pointed at Un-Deux-Trois.

"-do you people know how to fight a war? I mean, a real one; not just shooting warning shots at an unarmed ship. Against an enemy that has all this kind of stuff?"

He made a motion with his hands, indicating the Manyatta. The women shook their heads in unison once again.

"We do not fight. It is..." She fell silent, seemingly grasping for the right word. Finally she settled on, "Male."

He turned back to the old man lying helplessly on the ground, watching him intently. Mitchell wasn't eloquent. And his growing rage made it even more difficult than normal for him to find the right words. Still, he tried.

"Do you think this is just about the Maasai? About Mars? THEY'RE back. They're back! Like some kind of monster from an old children's story. They left us alone for a long, long time. But now they're back. Doing stuff like they used to do. But now they're going to do it in space as well. And other places."

Mitchell gestured as widely as his stubby arms would allow. It was a comical gesture and he knew it, but he couldn't control himself. "If you stay here and die then you can't fight the people who did this to you. You'll just be gone. And nobody else even knows how to use a spear. How are we supposed to fight them? We don't even know how to do that."

Mitchell sat back down, breathing hard. He wasn't absolutely sure but that was probably more words than he had ever spoken at one time in his entire life. The effort had been exhausting and he wasn't even sure he'd done a good job making his point. Or that he'd even told the entire truth, exactly. The "sisters" certainly knew how to use more than a spear and, from what he had heard of the Imazighen, they knew a lot more than that. But it was true in a greater sense. The Maasai seemed to him like they could fight a war if they had to, while most of the Children of the Nakba couldn't. He certainly knew he couldn't.

Surprisingly, the Doctor looked impressed. So did the trio of odd women. They stared at him for an uncomfortably long time, their identical expressions unfathomable to him, and then turned back to the old man.

"We will go with the Captain to get more of our sisters. Then we will help your entire colony get ready to go. Or is that not what you wish?"

"No. I wish to die here at home, not to become an impotent nomad wandering endlessly through space." Then he sighed. Or, more accurately, his AI sighed for him. "It probably doesn't matter anyhow. The Posthegemony ship is almost certainly faster, more powerful, and better armed than ours. We probably won't make it past the orbit of Deimos before it destroys us."

"Then we'll die trying." Mitchell sounded a lot braver than he actually felt. Mostly he was just tired and testy. "That's better than sitting her and watching all of you die not trying."

It was at that moment that Mars finally completed its rotation, bringing Arabia Terra, countless heads of alien cattle, the Manyatta, its slumbering inhabitants, doubtful leader, one overwhelmed captain with Down syndrome, three clones of a 20th Century French intellectual, and – perhaps most importantly – the *Andrew Levitz's* AI all into tightbeam range of the Downstar.

Nadine Mang: Asclepius, Deep Space

Captain Nadine Shu Tun Mang completed the Cosmic Consciousness Pose, and then folded herself into the lotus position on the floor of her cabin. The ironically named *Asclepius* thrummed about her, a living thing that enclosed her protectively within its mechanical innards. It was a familiar sensation, the high speed vibrating of the ship's four gyroscopic Volkov-Leshev drives. She's been feeling it nonstop for months now. Idly Mang wondered what it would be like to not feel the slight tremor throughout the cells of her body. Odd, probably.

She hated Tai Chi Chih. It was a useless, unproductive hippie-era waste of time in her opinion. A weird holdover from the early days of the Posthegemony when the Powers That Be were obsessing over the idea that someone, somewhere on the planet might learn a useful martial art. But it was expected that nomenklatura would practice the silly thing. So she did. It was always wise in her society to at least look like you were doing what was expected of you. Especially if you were part of the one-percent that pretended to run things – and, most especially, if you were part of the small percentage of that one-percent that happened to be female.

Her cabin was small and, by the standards of most people, extremely Spartan. There were no pictures of friends or family or lovers. No sentimental tokens of past adventures. Even the usual sweet of holographic projectors was absent. It was packed in the front of the ship adjoining the command center and the small clutch of cramped cabins, dining areas, science labs, and communication center that comprised the inhabited portions of the ship. Behind that was a large cargo bay, now mostly empty but once containing innumerable AI spy satellites, parasite tracking drones, smart missiles, and the other sundry accoutrements of modern warfare. And behind that, dwarfing all else, were the ship's drives.

Typically an earthbound AntiG craft contained two of these complex, expensive, and devilishly difficult to maintain machines: one to use and another for emergencies. Deviant spacecraft typically contained three: one to use, one spare, and one to maintain an Earth-normal gravity field within the confines of the ship. But the *Asclepius* had four: one for propulsion, one to provide the ship's internal gravity, and two in reserve should the craft need them, either for replacements or to provide a massive boost in propulsion.

Nadine Mang's ship was built for speed. In fact, it was probably the fastest craft ever created by mankind. Their slow, ponderous approach to the Downstar was deliberate. She hadn't wanted to alarm the retards or their keepers. She also hadn't wanted to broadcast the *Asclepius'* abilities before it was absolutely necessary. Its speed was a hidden advantage she planned on keeping hidden as long as she could possibly manage.

She smiled, looking directly at the only ornamentation at all in the room: her captain's commission from the Producer-Consumer Army Navy Space Command. A decade ago that would have meant that she spent her days as shuffling files in the morning, pleasuring her libido driven two-hundred-going-on-twenty boss in the afternoon, and being Ms. ArmCandy (snicker, snicker) to the same in the evening. Now it meant something very different indeed.

In fact, Nadine had removed anything from her cabin that might even for a moment dissuade her of the idea that she was living in a fragile, pressurized can hurtling through the void. She didn't want anything to distract her from that fact. She also didn't want anything to distract her from the fact that she was personally responsible for killing or forcibly converting countless thousands of people living in orbit around the Earth. She couldn't bring herself to think of them as "innocent" people. They were not innocent. (Though deep, deep down inside, where we are all forced to be honest with ourselves, she knew they were.) Furthermore, somewhere out there a historian – possibly one that wouldn't be born for hundreds of years – was going to give her a moniker like "The Butcher of Luna." It was inevitable at this point, and she simply had to accept it.

Why had she done it? The simple answer was that, when she had begun to compete with dozens of other promising nomenklatura for the position as captain of mankind's first legitimate interplanetary spacecraft, she had no idea that was what she would be asked to do. In a society with as little upward mobility as the Posthegemony – and as much pretense of compassion and civilization as the Posthegemony – one took whatever opportunities one could get and reasonably enough assumed they wouldn't have anything to do with genocide. But when she learned the true nature of her mission, she still didn't back down. After all, in an era that offered so little with which to distinguish yourself from the crowd, infamy could sound downright appealing.

And there was the not inconsiderable fact that it had to be done. Posthegemony society had been rocked to the core by the escape of the strange, dissident craft. Not so much because it had escaped as because it had existed at all. Its mere existence yanked something from the realm of the cryptozological and threw it right onto everyone's breakfast table, mewing and thrashing and drawing attention to itself. It was like walking around a familiar corner in your home Metro and finding Bigfoot doing a waltz with Cthulhu dressed in formal attire. Only on a planet wide scale. The result had been a societal temper tantrum, as if a particularly precocious and faithful child had suddenly realized – really realized, down to the core of her being – that there was no God. There had been riots, with crowds attempting to seize floaters, airtrams, airships: basically, anything that had a Volkov-Leshev AntiG drive in it and was roughly shaped like a spacecraft. And every nut job with a microgram of engineering ability had started constructing a capsule in his condo.

Across the web everyone everywhere suddenly became an expert on Interesting People: where they lived, who they were, what they did. And, more shockingly yet, how they might *become* one. fabers everywhere started churning out artifacts of a dubious and alarming nature. Prayer beads of many and various shocking varieties. Rosaries. Tasbih. Japa mala. African and Balinese household gods of a wild and erotic continence. Actual physical copies of ancient science fiction books by Heinlein, LeGuinn, and Rand. Toy weapons. Real weapons; though technically such a thing wasn't supposed to be possible. (But it turns out it was.) Orthodox icons. Dashboard ornaments. Matchbox cars. Solar panels. Action figures. Backpacks. Flashlights. Fetishes.

People began hording food. Drawing crude, kindergarten-level escape maps. Pulling away from one another and their carefully balanced communities, retreating to the familiar environs of their close friends and family. It was as if some great scab had been pulled off of society, allowing the puss and blood of madness to flow. Major Metros descended into chaos. Hoi-polloi assaulted post-polloi – and sometimes even nomenklatura. For months it seemed as though the world had gone mad, and was more than willing to toss aside a millennium of progress in an orgy of societal self-destruction.

But into this void stepped General Zhang Dakota Wannian. He was a whirlwind of organization, pulling the dazed fragments of Posthegemony society into his orbit like some massive Jovian world. His Space Command ceased being a secretive and bureaucratic documentary film crew armed with missiles, and began to emerge as an actual military force. The old RoboCop police androids, with their restrictive, anti-violent programming and limited AI, simply weren't able to handle the chaos of this new world. So Wannian recalled them and reactivated the actual Producer-Consumer Army. He began training humans to police other humans. He authorized the use of deadly force. He used carefully programmed and biologically targeted missiles to quell riots. He strategically shut down power to Scrapers and even whole sections of Metros, stopping insurrections before they could really start. He withheld food shipments to rebel neighborhoods, ruthlessly starving them back into compliance. (This didn't take long, as most Producer-Consumers considered going without food for 48 hours to be "starving.")

Nadine had come into her own during these Madness Times, cracking heads and quelling riots as a major in the PCA. It hadn't been pretty and it hadn't been fun. But for the first time in a thousand years, the governance of the Earth had been faced with a real crisis and it had persevered. What was more, it had created an entirely new class of people: those who had fought to put down the rebellion. And an entirely new place for them to be. The military. A place where a post-polloi like her could elevate her status to nomenklatura, and where the old class divisions didn't matter as much. It was also a place where producer-consumers who had been hardened by the experience of using violence on their fellow man could be separated from the common herd and, in turn find, camaraderie and understanding among people like themselves.

Conversely, the Madness Times had left society with an enormous population of malcontents. Far too many to be properly ReEducated without building entire Metros dedicated to the task.

Nadine understood that that idea had been seriously considered by the Powers That Be; as had other, even more drastic things she would rather not think about. But there had been another, less final solution. They needed somewhere to go. Somewhere more challenging that also separated them from their better, more innocent fellows.

They needed living room. Lebensraum. Spazio Vitale. And Nadine had supplied it in a matter of days: a feat unprecedented in human history.

She shook her head violently, clearing away old worries. None of that really mattered right now. What mattered was that the Downstar was on the move – and so was the *Andrew Levitz*. Now the question became which one to chase and capture or destroy. Or at least which one to do first. Both seem to be headed in the direction of 4 Vesta: a large asteroid belt planetoid that, from what she had learned from the near-Earth deviants, was inhabited by a rather large number of unpleasant, heavily armed people she would rather not tangle with at the moment. The ship's AI had determined this rather easily by triangulating their flight paths, and she had confirmed it through some fairly obvious guesswork. If she were one of the subhumans, wouldn't she want to run and hide beneath the skirts of someone vastly more superior?

At first glance the Downstar would be the obvious choice. It was almost twice as far from 4 Vesta as its daughter ship, and would have to move "downward" 1.3-degrees from its orbital inclination as well. It was also the second, carefully selected goal of her mission: a safe, easily secured base from which to launch the next step in civilizing the inner system. A forward position from which Earth could pacify Mars, Venus, Mercury, as well as any other miscellaneous orbital oddities like the station itself. Furthermore, it was necessary to secure the home world against aggression that came from "spinward" while the inner system was brought into civilization. The Downstar was ideal for that as well.

The *Andrew Levitz* in contrast was relatively close to 4-Vespa, and would only have to travel about .7-degrees "upward" to rendezvous with the tiny planet. It was also not part of her mission to capture or destroy it.

But now she wasn't so sure about the "easily secured" part of taking the Downstar. The station's exterior was made from portions of a small iron-nickel-basalt belt asteroid that had been further covered in carbon ice for radiation shielding. And, if the stations inhabitants could get it together enough to lock down the exterior thoroughly, it would take a small nuclear weapon to get inside. Which would defeat the point of taking it over, even if she possessed one. Which she didn't. And it was moving surprisingly quickly: almost three times as fast as their best estimates. Worse still, she wasn't 100% sure that the station wasn't armed. If it was, she knew that Cassidy Brazo wouldn't hesitate to fire upon her ship.

Damn. She thought. Who would have thought an actual retard could seize control of a space station?

She would have to go after the *Levitz*. The Downstar was filled with people that could still with a few notable exceptions be rehabilitated and uplifted into useful Posthegemony citizens through the application of modern medical science and a bit of persuasion. They were outcasts and defects, not rebels. The Maasai, on the other hand, would have to go. The historical record showed that they would never culturally evolve, no matter what the lure or threat. They hadn't back in the distant, quasi-medieval past of the S.A.C and they wouldn't now.

She rose and was reaching to touch the communication badge on her right breast when the voice of her second-in-command chimed through it.

"Captain Mang? Are you awake?"

She sighed. If she hadn't been before she certainly was now. That was obvious. Duke Hu Lan was an excellent first officer: diligent, intelligent, and utterly loyal. His "people skills" left a little to be desired, however.

"Yes commander? What is it?"

"There is a video broadbeam transmission from the Downstar," he sounded grim. "A powerful one. They're pumping everything they've got into it. It's being broadcast across all frequencies."

"Put it through to the smartscreen in my cabin."

"Aye captain."

A moment later the round, deceptively unintelligent-looking face of Cassidy Brazo appeared, looming huge and unnatural on one wall of her cabin. The "Special" Triumvir wore the distinctive Sentience Triumvir around her neck and Pablo Livni, the Standard representative, stood behind her with his hand on her shoulder. They were all dressed in their best clothing – garish, brightly colored track suits – and wore solemn, thoughtful expressions.

It would have been a touching scene of unity if it hadn't come from a group of people that were so obviously pathetic.

"Fellow Children," she began solemnly in her slightly impaired and lisping voice. "for those of you who have never heard of us, we are the ruling Triumvirate of Downstar Station: an orbital colony which has existed Antichthon to Earth for almost 800 years."

She smiled a little.

"For those who haven't... well, like a lot of you we keep to ourselves."

They've been coaching her, thought Mang. *And doing a good job of it too.*

"But all of that has changed now. And changed forever. Everything that was," she paused thoughtfully, "is now in the past. At the same time everything that was the past is now here. Because the Posthegemony has at last left Earth and has come for us all."

Damn. Nadine cursed. Pig bastard! That makes things more complicated.

Cassidy paused once again, then continued slowly and deliberately, pronouncing every syllable of Spanglanese with great care, a look of concentration on her face.

"You may have received a message several days ago from an AI claiming that it had attacked a Martian colony on behalf of Earth. That transmission was true. Earth has attacked a Maasai clan with a biological weapon that has altered their genes. This attack was deliberate, unprovoked, and cruel. We've evacuated that colony, and they are being taken to 4 Vesta for their own safety."

They're bating me. She realized suddenly. *Deliberately pointing me in the direction of the Berbers. Smart. Only they don't realize how fast we really are.*

"There is only one conclusion to be had from this: we are in a state of war with the Earth. It does not matter if if we want one. It does not matter if we know how to fight one. It does not matter that we don't understand why we are in one. What matters is that they have come for us, these monsters out of our ancestor's myths. They have come to destroy who we are and to take what we have built. And there is nothing we can do now but resist them with every fiber of our beings. This our sainted ancestors did, and we can do no less."

"At the end of this transmission you will find a compressed data packet containing a recording of the AI boasting about its attack, a report from one of our people from the surface of Mars, and a record of the conversations between myself and the captain of the Earth ship that launched this unprovoked attack. We think you fill find them... enlightening"

Nadine Mang winced at that.

"In conclusion, my name is Cassidy Eliza Brazo. I am the elected Special Triumvir on the Downstar Station. I am at war with the Earth. And, whether you know it or not, so are you. The sooner you come to understand this the more likely the Children of the Nakba – all Children of the Nakba – will survive the coming months and years."

The transmission ended, leaving Nadine Mang alone with her thoughts. At first she was filled with rage. *How dare that little bitch fuck with my plans like this? I'll get her if it's the last thing I do!*

Then she took a deep breath, exhaled slowly, and got control of herself.

Hookayyyy Nadine. Easy girl. This doesn't change anything.

And indeed it didn't. Somehow they'd managed to conquer or destroy the deviant near-Earth communities without any of the Children that lived farther out noticing. (She actually rather liked the sound of that phrase. Children. Because that's really what all of the deviants were, wasn't it? Children out in the wilderness, building forts and pretending to be adults?) That was partly due to excellent planning, but mostly just to dumb luck. And there was no way that luck could hold forever. True, it had run out a bit earlier than she would have liked. True, it had deprived the *Asclepius* of further diplomatic advantages that could be gained by the Children's ignorance of her true mission. But just the diplomatic ones.

Her military advantage was still very much in effect.

She stood, carefully straightened her uniform, placed her Sentience about her neck, and strode out of her cabin. A moment later she stood in the center of the ship's bridge, all eyes gazing upon her in the flickering, electronic light cast by the ship's control screens. She looked at each of her officers in turn, meeting those eyes with her own iron gaze.

"Mr. Lan, please bring Volkov-Leshev drive A – the one we're using for propulsion – to a halt. Slowly. I don't want to risk damaging it."

"Aye captain."

"When you've brought it all the way down, I want you to reorient it and C and D drives toward the sun. Correlate the drives with its magnetic field, and then slowly bring them up to full power. I want as much acceleration as you can give me. Without flattening all of us, of course.

Nervous laughter.

"Ms. Wei, please tell the torpedo room to prepare our remaining fish to go into the tubes. I want them to be ready to fire at a moment's notice."

"Aye captain."

"Mr. Xuan-Aldona, please consult the optics for the location of the *Andrew Levitz,* and then lay in an intercept course at greatest possible speed."

"Aye captain."

"Ladies, gentlemen, and artificial intelligences of all ages: we are going back to Mars."

Mitchell Green: Andrew Levitz, Near Mars Space

In the depths of space the *Andrew Levitz* was going hell bent for leather.

The ship sounded funny. Mitchell had turned on its backup drive in a desperate attempt to put as much distance between himself and the pursuing Posthegemony vessel as he possibly could. And now the familiar sounds and vibrations of his beloved ship were somehow wrong. Off. He had all three going – two of the engines for thrust, the third to protect its passengers from the forces of acceleration – and running the third engine made his familiar surroundings sound somehow alien. Like it was somebody else's ship.

The Sisters had been as good as their word. They'd come over the surface of Arabia Terra in large numbers, racing along in a caravan of ancient ground vehicles so weathered and beaten that it amazed him that all of them had actually made it. (Only later did it occur to him that many of them probably hadn't.) With great, oddly tender care they helped load all of the Maasai into the *Andrew Levitz's* shipping containers, carefully attaching nutrient drips to each of them so that they would remain hydrated and healthy during their trip to 4 Vesta. Then Un-Deux-Trois cocooned each one of them into emergency medical bags: silvery sacks that slowed the human metabolism to its lowest point possible ebb. Mitchell had seen them used before during medical emergencies on the Downstar. They were a pretty standard piece of Children tech; though the bags were used typically for temporary transport, and weren't designed for long term use. But they were the only appropriate thing the Sisters had in large quantities. He remembered wondering exactly how long they had been stored away within the depths of the small women's mysterious colony, and then deciding not to worry about it. They would work or they wouldn't. There was nothing in the big, cold universe he could do about it.

It had been his idea to route the bag's limited battery power supplies directly to the ship's hydrogen power plant, allowing them to function almost indefinitely. He was proud of that. Then he and the Sisters had strapped the Maasai to the floor of the containers with webbing so that wouldn't float around and hurt themselves if there was an emergency and he had to turn off or redirect the AntiG drive. Chicken, goat, cattle, and other embryos had been loaded into separate containers in cryogenic stasis containers, with the remaining livestock being taken by the Sisters as payment (and so that they wouldn't go to waste). Grass, grain, corn, and other types of seeds were loaded, as well as root-crop samples, tool schematics, fabers, the colony's AI, ancient books, clothing, spears – in short, anything that looked conceivably useful and would fit into the containers.

The Doctor had been put back under for the journey, but Sironka had been awoken and had joined Mitchell on the bridge, where he was comfortably strapped into a chair. As usual he was cheerful, despite being able to do little more than wiggle his fingers, smile or frown, and turn his head. But he could speak to Mitchell via the ship's AI by sub-vocalizing into a spare earbud that has been placed in his auditory canal, and seemed excited by the prospect of being in space.

And why not? Thought Mitchell, *He's never been here before. And it always excited me to go to Mars, after all.*

"Where are we now Traveler?"

"Somewhere between the orbit of Phobos and Deimos," Mitchell replied, pointing at a screen. "The ship's AI and my Sentience are trying to figure out the best way to use the ship's AntiG drives to get us away from Mars. They're trying to use the gravity of the planet, its moons, and the Sun to give us as much speed as possible."

"Oh?" The Maasai youth sounded intrigued. "How does that work, exactly?"

Mitchell considered trying to answer that question, then shrugged sheepishly. Why pretend to be something you aren't? "I honestly have no idea. They're a lot smarter than I am, and they think a lot faster than any human being can in any case."

Sironka nodded. "It takes a wise man to admit what he doesn't understand."

Mitchell blushed a little.

"When do we meet these... Imazighen?" he continued. "And who are they, exactly? We've never had any direct contact with them."

"As soon as we can," Mitchell peered at his screen, and then listened to his earbud for a moment, shaking his head. "Sentience isn't certain yet. They've sent two of their ships to meet us, but they aren't very fast. Big. Real big. But not fast."

"The Imazighen are... we'll, they're like us I suppose. They fled the Earth like all the other Children, and settled in the Belt. There are a lot of them, they're warlike, and they've never forgiven the Earth for forcing them out. Legends say they actually fought the Posthegemony even after what happened to the Pashtuns, and were the last ones to leave."

Mitchell shrugged.

"I'm not sure how much of that is true, actually. But everyone agrees they have weapons, and they hate the Earthers. And they have agreed to help us – even if it's just an excuse to attack the *Asclepius.*"

"Good enough for me." agreed the Maasai. "Do we have any weapons? Can we fight them as well?"

Mitchell shook his head.

"No. We don't have anything like that. All we can do it run away and hope they can't catch us... though they're definitely trying to. We're tracking them right now."

"Will they catch up with us before the Imazighen get to us?"

"Yes." Mitchell looked at his friend grimly. "They are moving very, very fast; much faster than we thought they could. They must have been holding back, faking their top speed when they were approaching the Downstar. It's like everything else about them: lies and misdirection and hidden threats."

Mitchell paused and the two of them sat in silence, the ship humming unnaturally around them.

"Sironka," he said at last, pulling the threads of his thoughts slowly together, "why is this happening? After all of this time, why are they here?"

His friend gingerly turned his head toward him.

"Traveler, I believe it has something to do with what lies at the core of civilization itself. With its sickness and obsessions, it's pride and arrogance. They have come for us because 'we' aren't part of 'them,' and must therefore either become 'them' – or not be at all. It is the basic drive of all civilizations, not just the Posthegemony. They are just the biggest, most recent, and most extreme example. To grow, assimilate, and dominate the world around them: or, in this case, worlds. That is what they do. To a so-called civilized person it's as basic as breathing or eating: they must control everything."

Mitchell nodded, but he didn't really understand. Wasn't he a "civilized" person? Wasn't Sironka? Their peoples wore clothing, used technology, and created art. Yet they had no desire to do any of these things. Maybe his friend meant something else. Maybe it was a word that Sentience wasn't translating very well. It wouldn't be the first time.

"I'm sure they tell themselves something else of course," he continued thoughtfully. "That they have come to help us. To 'civilize' us for our own good. Or maybe they believe that this is what they must do because they need our space and resources to expand. Which is mad. They obviously have no real conception of how vast, how truly enormous the solar system actually is. In a thousand years we haven't been able to consume a fraction of it. To say that there is room and resources for all is an understatement. It's as if the ancient Europeans landed and immediately decided that the most pressing and important thing to do was to capture Swaziland."

Mitchell had no idea what or where Swaziland had been. Presumably somewhere in Africa. But he had another idea.

"What if they simply can't understand?" he said. "How big it is, I mean. If I remember my ancient history they live their whole lives in huge cities. What if their minds just don't work that way anymore? What if they can't even imagine how big space is?"

"What if they..." he struggled for the words. "What if they can't look 'out' at all? Only... in. In at themselves, in at each other, and in at their cities? What if they can't see the outside as it exists at all? How big and perfect and beautiful it is. What if they don't really see us either?"

Sironka looked at him oddly. He must have gotten it all wrong.

"Sorry to interrupt," said Sentience is a tone of voice clearly indicating it wasn't. "But I have an incoming tightbeam transmission from the *Asclepius* for Mitchell. From Captain Mang to be specific."

Mitchell hesitated.

"Put her through." replied Sironka nodding at Mitchell, who reluctantly nodded back.

"Yes. Do it. Voice only."

"Putting the bitch through."

A moment later a soft ping in his inner ear indicated that they had been connected.

"This is Captain Green. What do you want?" He tried to sound brave. Or at least bored. But Mitchell knew that he just sounded scared.

"Captain is it?" She chuckled. It was a deep, sensual, somehow menacing thing. "They let you call yourself that little man? How... tolerant of them."

"What. Do. You. Want?" Now he just sounded pissed off.

"Your surrender." She on the other hand was really good at sounding bored. "Your girlfriend just declared war on the government. That makes your ship a pirate vessel and you a criminal in my book. So you can surrender, be boarded, and become prisoners of war. Or in one half an Earth standard hour I will, with great pleasure, blast you and your ship into so many atoms."

"You're not our government," he retorted.

"There is only one government, Mitchell. And I represent it. The sooner you retards figure that out, the better off you'll be."

The Special looked at his friend. The Maasai looked back and nodded.

"We won't surrender." he said at last.

"I was hoping you would say that."

Mitchell killed the connection.

"Well, that was pleasant." commented Sentience.

"Not really." The Special paused for a moment. "We definitely can't outrun them, can we ship?"

"No Captain." The AI typically didn't mince words when speaking with humans. "I have confirmed that with my radar and optical sensors."

"Well, we don't have to make it any easier for them." Mitchell reviewed his options. The *Andrew Levitz's* small fusion power plant couldn't run its two AntiG thrust engines any faster than it already was without tearing them apart. If he diverted his third engine from internal gravity generation to thrust he could definitely increase his speed, but only at the risk of crushing all of them. But if he didn't they were dead anyway. So why not?

Mitchell rose from his chair and walked over to Sironka. Gently he tightened the various straps on his friend's flight chair, buckling him in as firmly as possible. Then he returned to his own seat and repeated the process on himself.

"The other Maasai should be secure enough in the containers," he mused out loud to no one in particular. "Ship, divert all engines to thrust. Push it as far as you can without killing any of us right away."

"Yes Captain."

An instant later the sounds of the engines changed again, becoming even more "wrong" to Mitchell's trained ear than before. Then an enormous, invisible hand came down over his body, shoving him into the couch and crushing his personal Sentience painfully against his chest. He could hear Sironka groaning nearby.

"Tightbeam the Imazighen," he subvocalized between gritted teeth. "Tell them what we're doing. And tell them... tell them thank you."

"Aye, Captain." Sentience said without its usual hint of sarcasm. A moment later it added. "The Imazighen Sentience says they're coming as quickly as possible. If they cannot protect us, they promise to avenge us."

Mitchell didn't find that particularly comforting, but politely kept his opinion to himself.

"Then please connect me with the Downstar. I want..." his determination broke for a moment in the form of a small sob. Then he composed himself. "I want to say goodbye to Cassidy."

"Aye, Captain." A moment later, "I've contacted Triumvir Brazo's Sentience and will project a hologram of her shortly."

Tears welled up in Mitchell's eyes and were promptly forced backward away from his cheeks. He tried to gather his thoughts, tried to organize what he would say to his beloved. But in the end when her image appeared before him, hovering like a tiny, flickering doll above the keyboards and displays, all he could say was "I'm sorry Cassidy."

"Why?" She raised her hand as if to touch his face. "Why would you be sorry?"

"Because I'm not going to be there at our wedding." He started to laugh at the absurdity of the statement, but his chuckles quickly turned into choked sobs as the g-force pressed mercilessly down upon his chest. Composing himself, he saw that she was crying as well. Then he felt guilty.

"I can't surrender to them," he admitted when she was done, desperately trying to explain; to find the words that would make the wrenching pain of a lost future feel better somehow. To feel noble instead of just stupid. "We can't ever surrender to them. I can't outrun them and help is too far away. So dying is what they've left me."

"I know." Her voice was calm again but very hoarse, and it suddenly occurred to him that she'd been crying before he'd even called. *Of course,* he thought. Cass is plenty smart. Everybody on the station must have figured it out hours ago.

"I love you," he managed.

"I love you too. Mitchell, we should pray together. Pray for a miracle."

"Okay." He said lamely. He wasn't very religious, but he knew the words to the Prayer of Intercession. And under the circumstances it certainly couldn't hurt anything.

God, you created men in your image and intended for them to be free. We thank you for having granted to us the gift of your servants of life Saints Lejeune and Costa. They knew how to place their immense intelligence and deep faith the defense of our lives and freedom, always seeking to protect and guide us. Witnesses to truth and love, they knew how to reconcile faith and reason in the face of oppression. By their intercession, and according to your will, we ask you to save us and divert away the fate which lies before us. Amen.

He wasn't sure that praying to the men whose work had led to the medicines that made his life possible actually helped. But it made him feel a little better. And it definitely made Cassidy feel better.

"And now for a miracle," he whispered.

"Yes," she replied faintly, "now for a miracle."

Mitchell cut the connection. For a few moments neither Special nor Maasai nor Sentience nor ship said anything. Then Sironka smiled, turning his head toward his friend with obvious effort.

"Beautiful," he said. "Simply beautiful Traveler."

"Well, it may not be a miracle, but I have an idea," interjected Sentience. "It probably won't save us, but it won't make like any easier for the bitch in that boat, I promise you that."

"Well don't keep it to yourself machine." The Maasai sounded almost amused. "Share it with the whole village."

"Let's take the *Andrew Levitz* down to Deimos," it suggested. "We're about to pass close to it right now, and changing our coarse by a few thousand kilometers shouldn't cost us more than a few minutes. We can skim along the surface at a distance of five or ten meters, dodging rock formations and dipping into craters as we go. It should play hell on their ship's sensors and make it harder for their missiles to lock onto us."

"Then if we're lucky," it continued, "we can slingshot around the back at an unpredictable angle using the moon's gravity to augment our engines. We'll be going fast. Very fast. We still won't make it to 4 Vesta or our rendezvous with the Imazighen ships. And you organics will probably all be crushed. But so what? If we're not going to survive, we might as well make her burn fuel. And time. As much as possible. Maybe enough for the Downstar to reach the belt and the Imazighen to make Mars orbit before she can get away."

"I like it," murmured Sironka, "A good death."

"I'd like living a lot more," sighed Mitchell. "But since I can't have that, I'll have to settle for being a pain in the ass instead."

Nadine Mang: Deimos Orbit

Deimos was the smaller and more distant of Mars' two moons: a giant, potato-shaped rock moving alone through the darkness of space. It was covered with small craters, blocks of regolith, and the remains of settlements so long abandoned that none of the living Children even remembered who had once lived there.

Or at least none of the ones she'd killed so far had.

Nadine Mang had watched with incredulity as the *Andrew Levitz* plunged toward the surface of the tiny dead planet without slowing, expertly finishing a broad turn to skim along its surface with surprising deftness as it negotiated into depressions and between obstacles. She rested her delicate chin thoughtfully upon clinched fist, shifting slightly in her command chair.

"Mr. Lan, what kind of fish do we have left in our locker? Are we in range?"

She winced inwardly at the use of the ancient nautical term, but what could she do? The Earth had to build a space fleet from scratch, and the references to actual space travel in the Posthegemony's vast databases were shockingly small considering that an enormous portion of the human race resided in space.

"Three dozen smart AI-equipped high explosive missiles for attacking ships." he replied, "Plus a dozen dumb kinetic energy penetrators for striking settlements from orbit and a couple of nanovirus equipped parachute bombs that haven't been programmed for any particular genetic type at this point. And, yes mam, we are.""Well, the last two aren't going to do us any good." She mused. "And we don't want to use too many of our high explosive fish in case we run into our good friends the Berbers, now do we? So send three their way right now please – straight down upon their heads."

"Aye Captain."

Mitchell Green: Deimos Surface

Mitchell had never seen a fox or a hound. He had, however, seen an ancient cartoon about the two, and remembered wondering how the fox must have felt as the hounds chased it through the animated thickets, bent upon taking its life.

He didn't wonder any longer.

Meters above the surface of Deimos the *Andrew Levitz* ducked and weaved at high speeds, desperately attempting to shake off the doom which doggedly pursued it. The grating sounds of electronic voices shrieked in his earbud, seemingly from inside of his brain, as his Sentience and the ship's AI waged their own war against the three missiles that pursued them. Taunting. Insulting. Distracting. Attempting to confuse and discourage. Looking for opening in their electronic defenses through which viruses, Trojans, and worms could slink through to do their dirty digital deeds.

Mitchell felt the beginnings of another headache at the edge of his consciousness, but forced it away through a sheer act of will. He wasn't going to die with a headache.

The three missiles had come screaming down on top of them, expected yet somehow still unexpected, minutes before. They were chemically propelled: hot, intense dots against the greens, grays, and blacks of his display screens. Deadly. Fast. And oddly unconcerned with their own mortality, given that they were self-aware.

"Voltaire Crater coming up in fifteen seconds Captain." The AI sounded unusually calm.

"Take us into it." Mitchell replied. "Any luck screwing with the missiles?"

"No," replied Sentience. "They are singularly unimaginative. But their software is well-defended."

"Too bad. Who was Voltaire, anyhow?"

"A cynical French satirist who attacked optimism and felt the human condition to be basically hopeless."

"Oh." Mitchell was sorry he'd asked.

There was a sudden, sickening sensation as the *Andrew Levitz* plunged over the side of the crater, dropping suddenly downward before leveling out once again. This was followed by a series of terrible grinding sensations as the ship deliberately tapped the lowest of its shipping containers against the surface of the tiny moon, sending massive clouds of dust upward in its wake. The idea is that they would confuse the missiles' sensors, hopefully causing them to slam into something.

"Exiting Voltaire Crater Captain."

There was an equally sickening sensation at the ship shot almost vertically upward, leaping over the lip of the crater and almost immediately dodging a boulder nearly as big as itself. However, shortly afterward there was the inspiring sight of one of the red blips disappearing from his screens. Sironka whooped with glee.

"One missile destroyed Captain. Entering Swift Crater in ten seconds."

"Okay, I'll bite," interjected Sironka. "Who was Swift?"

"An Irish satirist who advocated that poor people should sell their own children for food."

"Who in the hell was in charge of naming these things?" demanded Mitchell.

"Astronomers," replied Sentience. "They didn't get out much."

The ship plunged into the Swift Crater wish another sickening lurch, the two remaining red blips hot on its tail. It was beginning to execute another "butt in the dust" maneuver when all of Mitchell's screens began to flash red in alarm simultaneously.

"Danger! Unknown ship detected dead ahead! Prepare for extreme maneuvers!"

The ship slammed upward, g-forces driving Mitchell into his command chair so hard that he felt the emergency crash bags inflating around him in a cloud of choking, powdery chemicals and blinding pain. He caught a glimpse of an enormous shape passing across the ship's rear external display screen before the darkness took him, mercifully yanking him out of a sea of agony and plunging him into the warm, unknowing darkness.

Damn if it didn't look just like a giant silver woman.

Elvis Aaron Presley: Deimos Orbit

The humannequin known as Elvis Aaron Presley shot up from the surface of Deimos at speeds that would have turned the bones of an organic being to so much pulp, humming pleasantly to himself as he heaved the massive bulk of the *Gilda* into the path of the two missiles that pursued the Andrew Levitz. They detonated, blowing away sections of the ship's BioCrete hull and depressurizing entire decks in a spectacular spray of golden debris.

No matter. Elvis didn't mind.

He chuckled and continued humming as numerous warning lights flashed red and shocking on all of the screens of his dashboard. His knuckles tightened, gripping a wheel that wouldn't have been out of place in a pre-S.A.C sports car. Because, as far as he could tell, it was one.

And it wasn't like the ship was going to survive this little joyride in any case.

Of course the control room didn't exist anywhere outside of his own Hebbian neural networks, and his actual body lay in a womb of steel and titanium in the heart of the proud, sexy girl like an unborn mechanical child. Again: no matter. For the moment the ship was his body, even though he didn't like to conceptualize it that way. It felt unnatural, not to mention more than a little painful. Better to conduct the whole thing from the seat of his racecar from Speedway. He'd liked that movie. He'd liked the car too: a fastback Dodge Charger with a 426 Hemi "Elephant" V-8 engine in it. Rippin! It made him feel like singing while he drove.

A little less conversation, a little more action please!
All this aggravation ain't satisfaction in me
A little more bite and a little less bark
A little less fight and a little more spark
Close your mouth and open up your heart and baby satisfy me
Satisfy me baby

Better tightbeam the boys on the Andrew Levitz before they do something stupid and get themselves killed anyhow, he thought. A moment later he had their ship on the line.

"This is the free ship *Gilda,*" he announced. "We'll be handling the little matter of the Posthegemony vessel, so why don't you boys take your precious cargo and scamper off now. Your friends are waiting for you."

He was alarmed when only the ship itself seemed to be able to respond. Had he been too late? Had the shock wave from the exploding missiles somehow killed all of them, despite his efforts?

"Understood." Ship's AI's weren't what you would call imaginative, but this one added. "I will move my passengers to safety. And thank you whoever you are. Good luck."

That would have to do. He broke the connection, squared his handsome jaw, and pushed the pedal all the way down to the floorboard.

Nadine Mang: Deimos Orbit

"What. In. The. Hell. Is. That?" Nadine Mang screamed, beating her fist repeatedly against the arm of her command chair. Of course she knew what it was, and everyone else on the bridge knew she knew what it was too. The dissident ship. The enemy. THE enemy. The one that had plunged her society in chaos, destroying her little girl world and remaking her into the woman she had become: The murderer. The Butcher of Luna. It was the enemy that has propelled Zhang Dakota Wannian to predominance, and forced humanity to return to the stars. It was, in a very real sense, the pivot upon which modern history had turned.

She supposed she should thank it. Instead, she was going to kill it.

Weirdly an image flashed uninvited into her mind. It was an old pre-S.A.C show she used to watch as a child in her mother's condominium; an anime cartoon from old Japan that starred a one-eyed pirate captain. He was always holding a glass of red wine in his right hand, even when fighting his enemies in massive space battles. But he never seemed to get drunk. And when he became enraged, he threw the glass against the bulkhead, shattering it, and then stood up to shout orders.

She wished she had a glass to shatter. But she didn't. So she'd have to settle for just standing up and shouting orders.

"Fire everything!" she screamed, pointing at Lan. "Fire all remaining explosive missiles! Then throw all of the kinetic energy penetrators at it! Maybe they'll get lucky and hit it too. Use everything – every last fish. Climb into the tube and fire yourself at it if you have to!"

"Aye Captain," replied Lan unflappably. He probably would too. Idiot.

Elvis Aaron Presley: Deimos Orbit

The *Gilda* wasn't armed. She didn't need to be. Massive, powerful, heavily armored, and designed for a crew more-or-less immune to the stresses of g-force, she was built to run not fight. And that was exactly what Elvis intended to do: run her straight at the *Asclepius*. Straight into the thing that symbolized everything that he had come to despise.

He hummed happily to himself, thinking about his proxy life. About Priscilla and Natalie and Nancy and Anne and Elvira and Cybill and all the good times they'd had. The whole big, sordid, mythological life of a soiled messiah that wasn't really him, but at the same time was. All beautiful and complete, right down to his druggie martyrdom on the john.

Missiles seemed to be detonating everywhere at once, biting into the *Gilda's* flesh and sending flaming chunks of her BioCrete exterior tumbling back toward the surface of the tiny moon. Some sort of massive kinetic weapon tore straight through her, ripping apart one of the engines in the process. Ensconced in his own virtual reality, it felt like the Dodge's engine had thrown a rod.

It was a beautiful thing to behold, had there been anyone there to behold it. The golden woman charging up through space like a super heroine, battered but defiant, intent on saving the world from evil. The spacecraft blazing away at her with a shower of deadly explosions like the wrath of an ancient, primordial god. The rock star gripping the wheel of his expensive racecar, grinning through the pills and booze even as he plunged – willingly, knowingly – off of a cliff and into legend. The supermodel beauty freaking out on the stage like a three-year-old, screaming at her cringing lackeys, oblivious to the fact that the whole thing was being caught on video, broadcast to the entire world, and that it would humiliate her for the rest of her life.

And there was nothing any of them could do to avoid their fate. Ever.

Beautiful, beautiful, beautiful, thought Elvis, even as the *Gilda* slammed straight into the hull of the *Asclepius*, producing one of the most awe-inspiring non-nuclear explosions in human history.

AFTERWORD

There were times when Pablo Livni wished he could "un-learn" things. For example, he could have died a happy, old Standard never having known that the woman he had agreed to allow onto his home (at least in holographic form) had been responsible for butchering or enslaving the countless thousands of innocent Children in their orbital habitats around Terra. He certainly could have gone to the next life without becoming involved in a war, or learning about the strange fate of humanity on its birth world.

Still, as the old saying went: God does not call the equipped, He equips the called. Or so Pablo hoped. Because with the exception of the exceedingly, disturbingly equipped Imazighen, nobody in the solar system was ready for a fight. In fact, he couldn't think of a group of people less ready than the inhabitants of the Downstar.

"We are entering Deimos orbit," said the ludicrously beautiful redhead seated to his right. He sighed. She wasn't really a woman, of course. She was a kind of robot. And from what she (or possibly it) had told the Triumvirate, the Maasai clan leaders, and exotic and frightening queen of the Imazighen, she was in a very real way responsible for what had happened to those murdered thousands and the crippled Maasai. Possibly she was even responsible for starting the war with Earth. After all, if she and her kind hadn't insisted on making such a spectacle of themselves, the Posthegemony would still be peacefully slumbering the sleep of the decadent and damned.

Still, it was hard to be mad at her. She was so... well, hot. And, ultimately, weren't men responsible for their own actions? Even the Terrans?

"The Imazighen ships are leaving to establish a defensive orbit around Mars." She deftly adjusted the controls on the panel in front of her; though it must have been maddeningly slow for a being used to doing the same thing at the speed of thought, he reflected. He glanced at his own screen, watching as the menacing cylinders slid away from the *Jason Kingsly* and toward the red giant below. The Berbers called them "pipe ships," and the name made sense. They like giant sections of pipe. Except that they bristled with mysterious weapons of all kinds at every angle, most of whose deadly purposes he couldn't even begin to guess at. But even the poor old *Jason Kingsly* was armed now, it's peaceful shipping containers replaced with racks of missiles and Gauss rifles marring its stubby, rounded wings.

Not that he minded. Especially considering what has happened to her sister ship.

The *Andrew Levitz* had limped into orbit around 4 Vesta a week after the Downstar had arrived, crew and passengers half-dead from the injuries they'd sustained escaping from the surface of Deimos and all but one of its AntiG engines burned out from constant acceleration. The force had broken most of Mitchell and Sironka's ribs, and the rest of the Maasai hadn't fared much better. They were all recovering aboard the Downstar, to which the Alliance had assigned the role of hospital station.

The Alliance. Pablo forced himself not to sigh again. That was what they were calling themselves, this wary coalition of paranoid Berbers, renegade robots, infected Maasai tribesmen, and, of course, his people.

Well, we have to call ourselves something, didn't we? He reflected ruefully.

"Scanning with optical sensors, radar, and high frequency radio," she continued. "Rita" and her people had shown up shortly after the *Andrew Levitz* in their new ship the *Durand Durand.* Apparently, the Earth hadn't considered the Amors close enough to be included in its initial onslaught, giving their inhabitants enough time to flee toward the belt. He had a feeling that was an oversight the Posthegemony was going to live to regret. As it was, the now-destroyed *Gilda* has tracked the *Asclepius* from a distance ever sense the attack, skulking about and looking at a chance for revenge. And it had found one. But if the Terran crew and their captain hadn't been so incredibly arrogant, the humannequin ship probably never would have gotten that chance.

Rita placed her hand on his arm. It was surprisingly warm.

"I've detected a weak radio signal coming from an object about two thousand yards to port," she murmured, the corners of her incredibly perfect mouth curling upward in pleasure. "Would you like to hear it?"

He nodded, his earbud suddenly filling with music.

A little less conversation, a little more action please!
All this aggravation ain't satisfaction in me
A little more bite and a little less bark
A little less fight and a little more spark
Close your mouth and open up your heart and baby satisfy me
Satisfy me baby

Come on baby I'm tired of talking
Grab your coat and let's start walking
Come on, come on
Come on, come on
No procrastinating, don't articulate
Girl it's getting late, you just sit and wait around

A little less conversation, a little more action please!

About the Author

Jason S. Walters is an author, essayist, and publisher best known for running Indie Press Revolution (IPR), a distributor of micro-published roleplaying games. He is also one of a small group of investors that purchased Hero Games in 2001, and serves as its general manager. After owning a San Francisco bike messenger service for 15 years, he and his wife Tina moved to Midian Ranch: a homestead near the town of Gerlach, Nevada. It is also the location of IPR's warehousing complex. They have a daughter with Down syndrome named Cassidy and animals too numerous to mention.

by Jason Walters

Highdome and his crew of cutthroats, monsters, and mutants don't care. They just want to stay alive. But when sorcery backfires and the fury of the Vast White desert is unleashed, the men of the Red Regiment must look inside of themselves to find the strength to survive.
[Dark Fantasy, ages 14+]

by Jason Walters

This collection of horrific short stories from Nevada's Black Rock Desert will give you nightmares for years to come. The very landscape of the desert it portrays seems to have a will of its own, as if possessed by a violent, hideous determination to purge all visitors from its bosom. It suffers only those few who need nothing.
[Horror Short Stories, ages 18+]